W9-BTQ-338

HENRY *of* ATLANTIC CITY

HENRY *of* ATLANTIC CITY

FREDERICK REUSS

MACMURRAY & BECK
DENVER

Copyright © 1999 by Frederick Reuss
Published by:
MacMurray & Beck
Alta Court
1490 Lafayette, Ste. 108
Denver, CO 80218

Excerpts, as submitted, from THE NAG HAMMADI LIBRARY IN ENGLISH,
3RD, COMPLETELY REVISED ED. by JAMES M. ROBINSON, GENERAL
EDITOR. Copyright © 1978, 1988 by E.J. Brill, Leiden, The Netherlands.
Reprinted by permission of HarperCollins Publishers, Inc. For additional
territory contact Koninklijke Brill NV, Plantijnstrasse 2, Postbus 9000,
2300 PA, Leiden, The Netherlands.

Printed and bound in the United States of America

1 2 3 4 5 6 7 8 9 10

Reuss, Frederick, 1960–
Henry of Atlantic City / by Frederick Reuss.
p.   cm.
ISBN 1-878448-89-7
I. Title.
PS3568.E7818H46   1999
813'.54—dc21   99-26946
                                              CIP

MacMurray & Beck Fiction: General Editor, Greg Michalson
Henry of Atlantic City cover design by Laurie Dolphin.
The text was set in Weiss by Chris Davis, Mulberry Tree Enterprises.

For my family

1

BYZANTIUM

Mrs. O'Brien was a fat woman with red hair and a red face and two sides to her that Henry saw the minute his father drove off in the Maserati Quattroporte he'd won in a bet. She was all smiles when other people were around but when they were alone she turned into a witch. Mr. O'Brien worked at night somewhere. Henry never knew exactly where, but it must have been a salt mine or a steel factory because Mr. O'Brien was the tiredest, dirtiest man Henry had ever seen. Henry was always glad when he turned up. When Mrs. O'Brien yelled, Mr. O'Brien would tell her to shut up.

Before he was left at the O'Briens', Henry lived in Philadelphia with Sy's sister. Before *that* he lived with his father in Caesar's Palace. The Palace was always busy. People said you could hear the noise from the slot machines as far away as Smyrna, which was all the way in Delaware. But even if that wasn't true and you could only hear them as far as Cologne—which was halfway to Philadelphia—

that was *loud*. Caesar's Palace was big and people came from all over to play. Henry's father was chief of security. It was sort of like being quaestor of the Sacred Palace and captain of the Blues rolled into one. The Byzantine historian Procopius wrote a lot about the Blues—not the music but one of the teams that ran in the chariot races in the Hippodrome. In the olden days most of the people in Byzantium were Blues, but there were many Greens too. Procopius said Byzantium was the city where the east toucheth the west. That made it special. When Henry read the old historian's books he decided he wanted to live there—not just in Byzantium but in a place where things touchethed like that—east and west, waves and shore, light and dark, past and present. To be in between two touching things meant you were on the spot where they came together. It meant they came together in you, and after all Henry had seen and read and been through, he couldn't think of anything better than that.

Being chief of security was like living where things come together too—like where a rock toucheth a hard place. That's what Henry's father said all the time after Theodora became general manager of the Palace. Theodora was also the name of the Emperor Justinian's wife, and being general manager of Caesar's Palace was sort of like being an empress. Henry's father was six feet tall and weighed one hundred ninety-one pounds, so for him being between a rock and a hard place was not very comfortable. There were nights when he came off work so tired that he fell asleep right on the sofa holding a bottle of beer in his hand. Even if Henry took off his shoes and socks and tickled his feet he wouldn't wake up. The only thing that could wake him up was his beeper. When that went off he always said, "Jesus Christ," because it meant there was trouble. There was always some kind of trouble going on. Henry liked to go and watch whenever he could. You had to be a grown-up to go most places in the Palace, but that didn't stop Henry. He knew how to sneak into the Bacchus Room and the Gladiator Lounge and had even been backstage at the Forum. His father said he didn't know what was harder, keeping his job or keeping up with Henry.

Then one day his father took him out on the beach. It was the beginning of the summer, and the city was getting crowded. It was the first time Henry had ever been on the beach with his father—or even seen him wearing swimming trunks. He always dressed in suits because that's how chiefs of security have to dress. It was hot. They walked and walked, past Balley's Wild West and Trump Plaza and the Tropicana and the Taj, past the pier with the Ferris wheel at the end, past everything and everybody until they were alone and there was no one else. Finally his father said, "It's time to get you out of here, kid. Time to go to school." He picked Henry up and put him on his shoulders and they walked for a little while longer. "First you're going to spend the summer with Sy's sister. She lives in Philly." Then he put Henry down. "You're gonna love her, kid." He took his gold chain off and put it around Henry's neck, then picked Henry up again and put him back on his shoulders. "That's so you have something to remember me by," he said, and they headed back to the Palace. "I don't want you to worry, kid. No tears. Everything's gonna be fine." Then he had to put Henry down because his beeper went off.

The summer went by fast and slow at the same time, and even though they didn't fall in love, Henry liked Sy's sister a whole lot. She was older than Sy and lived in a row house that had stained-glass windows that were left over from her hippie days. In the morning when you came downstairs the living room was filled with colored light. It looked sort of like the pictures in the book about the Hagia Sophia, and in the fall, when his father brought him to the O'Briens', Henry brought that book with him to remind him of Sy's sister and her house. Of all the things he did that summer, getting books out of the Philadelphia Public Library had been the funnest. It wasn't stealing, either. It was called borrowing.

He was sent to Catholic school. His father said it would be good for him. He never said why. Henry figured that it was all very complicated and probably had to do with appearances. He had learned all about appearances that summer. Henry was a gnostic. He said so on the playground and in religion class and Sister Theresa told the principal, Sister Agnes Mary, who took him over to the rectory. "We'll just see what Father has to say about these silly stories of yours, young man," she said. "Idle minds are the devil's workshop." Henry could tell she was angry because she was pretending not to be.

Father Crowley had lots of silver hair and dark eyes that made him look tired. Sometimes he wore a black suit and sometimes he wore a black cassock but he never wore a hat. The priest said he wanted to hear all of Henry's story, so on Saturday he came to the O'Briens' house in his black Chevrolet Malibu that said CLERGY on the license plate and talked with Mrs. O'Brien. She became a jolly fat lady as soon as the priest walked into the house. She put her arm on Henry's shoulder and squeezed him against her thigh and talked a lot and forgot to breathe. Henry could tell when Mrs. O'Brien forgot to breathe because her face got red and she made a wiggling motion and said, "Lord, oh Lord!" all the time. Father Crowley and she agreed that the best thing would be for Henry to spend the day at the rectory, where they could have a quiet talk. Mrs. O'Brien said, "Don't you worry about the time, Father. I'll keep his dinner warm."

On the way to the rectory Father Crowley pulled into a shopping center that had a Baskin Robbins. "I love ice cream," he said. "Care to join me for a dip?" He laughed.

Henry went inside with the priest and asked for Rocky Road because that was what he felt like. When they returned to the car Father Crowley didn't drive but sat behind the wheel licking his ice cream cone and frowning. Henry licked his too and watched out his window as cars turned in and out of the parking lot.

Then the priest turned to him. "So, Henry," he said. "Where did you hear about gnosticism?"

Henry said Philadelphia.

The priest's cone dripped and he wiped the ice cream from his lap. Henry began to tell him about *veneranda vetustatis auctoritas*, which means the venerable authority of antiquity, and the gnostic secrets he'd learned in *The Coptic Gnostic Library* and about Procopius and *The Secret History* and about the Hagia Sophia and the Blues and the Greens and his friends Helena—whose mother was the Whore of Jersey City—and Sy.

Henry missed Helena. He missed Sy and the Palace too. He wanted to go back but his father told him it was impossible because he didn't know who his friends and who his enemies were anymore. He said real friends were the people you did things with that you didn't want anyone else to know about. Real friends were very rare and only came along once or maybe twice in a whole lifetime and you always knew where you stood with them. The only problem was that the same was true for enemies. You always knew where you stood with them too, and things could get real dangerous when you didn't know and weren't sure. Theodora was one of those people who was hard to figure out. She was a powerful bitch.

"Hey, hey, hey," Father Crowley said. "You watch your language, young man." He dripped more ice cream into his lap and said, "Oh gosh," and got a napkin out of the glove box.

Anyway, Henry's father was never sure where he stood with her. He said that one day when everything settled down they would move to an island somewhere far away and buy a houseboat where Henry and he would live together. Henry made him promise and he said, "Kid, if things go according to plan we'll be able to do anything. You name it."

"When did he tell you all these things, Henry?" Father Crowley asked.

Henry said he didn't remember.

"Was it in Atlantic City?"

Henry nodded.

When they got to the rectory, Father Crowley took Henry to a big, sunny room with a couch and some tables and chairs. It looked like a card room without the card table and there was a whole wall with books. It reminded him of the library near Sy's sister's store in Philadelphia except there was a fireplace with a crucifix over it. Father Crowley wanted Henry to tell him more.

The Whore of Jersey City lived next door to Henry and his father at the Palace. They called her the Whore of Jersey City because once she was in a movie called *The Whore of Jersey City*. Helena was her daughter. Jersey City worried about her hair too much. She made Ruben come up to her apartment at least once a week and sometimes even more than that. Ruben was a hairdresser from Bethlehem and he did everyone's hair if they were famous because somehow he was famous too. Jersey City had been in more

than ten movies and that's why *she* was famous. Helena
went to a college up in the mountains. Not the Carpathi-
ans or the Caucasus or the Alps, but mountains like them
somewhere in New Hampshire. Jersey City was very proud
of her. When she came home after the first semester, she
hardly ever left the apartment and her mother told Henry's
father that she had become a real snoot and was always ar-
guing and they were driving each other crazy.

Helena used to take Henry out to the beach. She was
eighteen and had light brown hair and blue eyes that gave
her a faraway look. She was pretty and whenever people
told her so she got mad. It happened all the time on the
beach. One day she brought a book with her called *Huckleberry Finn* that starts like this: *You don't know about me, without you have read a book by the name of The Adventures of Tom
Sawyer, but that ain't no matter. That book was made by Mr. Mark
Twain, and he told the truth, mainly. There was things which he
stretched, but mainly he told the truth.*

The priest sat up in his chair. "That's very good,
Henry. Did you memorize that all by yourself?"

Henry nodded.

"Well, now, I have a suggestion. Instead of talking
about gnosticism and things you're too young to understand, how about telling the story of Huckleberry Finn?
The sisters might not mind that."

Henry said yes, they would mind, because when Sister
Helene heard him on the playground she was all smiles at
first but when he got to the part where it went, *After supper*

she got out her book and learned me about Moses and the Bulrushers and I was in a sweat to find out all about him but by-and-by she let out out that Moses had been dead a considerable long time so then I didn't care no more about him because I don't take no stock in dead people—when that happened she made him stop.

"I see," said the priest and touched the tips of his folded hands to his lips like he was going to say prayers.

Reading was easy. Helena showed Henry how to do it right out there under the umbrella on the beach. Pretty soon he could do it without moving his lips. Helena said he was smart because he learned without her even having to teach him. They got to be real good friends and pretty soon Henry read to her when they were on the beach and even when they weren't on the beach they did stuff together. Like one day when they dumped a glass of milk out a window right on a man Helena hated because he was hanging around her mother. They ran down the back stairs and all the way to Sy's place. That was how Henry learned about plague sowing.

Father Crowley shook his head. "You're going too fast, Henry. Slow down."

Henry talked about Chryssomallo, who used to be a dancer and a lion tamer and who wrestled with other women gladiators in the Forum but quit and became a bodybuilder, a fortune-teller, and a healer. People went to her to ask for help all the time. She was a friend of the Whore of Jersey City from the old days and Helena said they were in some movies together. You could go to her and for twenty-five dollars she would stand in front of you for ten minutes and flex her muscles. People went to her for healing. Next to Theodora, Henry figured she was one of the busiest women in Byzantium.

"Byzantium?"

Henry nodded and explained that it was the capital of the eastern empire and that there were Trojans in the Palace because of AIDS. Not people from Troy—*rubbers.*

Father Crowley looked like he was going to get mad but he didn't. Henry explained that there were machines in all the bathrooms. Trojans made good plague sowers and Henry dropped them off the roof of the Palace for fun. He pretended that each Trojan was filled with plague germs and when it hit the ground, whoever got splashed would get the plague.

There was another way of plague sowing that was even more fun. Helena taught him. You took a Trojan and put some half-and-half coffee creamer into it. Then when nobody was looking you left it someplace—like in a corridor or on a chair in the lobby. Henry did a lot of plague sowing around the Palace until Theodora made the Palace guards do extra shifts walking the corridors and checking the chairs in the lobby and the staircases. That was just before the Nike riots happened and they had to go to Sy's sister's house in Philadelphia.

"Nike riots?"

Henry explained that he meant the Greek goddess of victory, not the running shoes. Procopius said that Cappadocian John was responsible and the riots started after a Blue and a Green were hung for treason and the rope broke. A miracle of God had saved the two men but the emperor refused to pardon them and so the factions burned and looted and killed. Byzantium was nearly destroyed.

"That's all very interesting, Henry," the priest cut in. "Let's see. Why don't you tell me about Theodora?"

Henry didn't want to talk about Theodora. He was scared of her. His father told him to stay out of her way and not to do anything that made her mad or unhappy. "She could put us out on the street in a minute," he told Henry. There were other things he said too, but they mostly had to do with his job as chief of security or his work with Sy, which had to do with siphoning or skimming, Henry wasn't sure which. All Henry knew for sure was that his father hated Theodora. One time he heard him talking to Sy: "She's squeezing me to *death*. Doesn't come out and say it. Just drops hints here and there. And those fucking *looks!* I'm tired of it. Tired of fucking tiptoeing. She wants me to think I owe her big time." Sy said, "You do." Henry's father got mad and started yelling, "I don't owe nobody *nothin'!* Understand? I do what I want. Nobody owns me, mister! No smart-ass MBA bitch. *Nobody!*"

Theodora swam every morning in the Palace's Olympic swimming pool. Sometimes Henry would hide and watch. She was tall and thin and her hair was short and very dark and her skin was very white. She would come out of the women's shower room and hang her towel on the back of a chair. She always wore a purple bathing suit that had a black stripe up the side that made her legs look very long. She put on a small purple cap and tucked her hair up into it as she walked to the edge of the pool. She always bent down once or twice to touch her toes. Then she would dive in. She swam very slowly—on her stomach, on her back, on her side, and underwater. Her arms would come out of the water lazily and slide back in and she kicked her feet without splashing. She moved through the water quickly and quietly and left a little bubbly wake behind her. When she reached the end of the pool she flipped, rolled, and resurfaced. She would blow a fine spray of mist into the air, then disappear again into the deep. Procopius said that when Justinian was emperor, a whale lived in the straits of the Bosphorus. People called it Porphyrius because it looked like it was made of the same purple stone as the great column in the Forum of Constantine. The whale lived in the waters around the city for a long, long time and sailors said they saw her as far away as the Black Sea. Theodora was a very good swimmer, and she was the most beautiful woman in the world.

"I'm waiting," the priest said. "What can you tell me about Theodora?"

Henry said Theodora was the wife of the Emperor Justinian. Procopius called Justinian and Theodora demons in human form.

"Okay," Father Crowley said. "What about Sy? Who is Sy?"

Sy's real name was Simon. He was a Jew from Babylon, the one on Long Island, not the capital of Babylonia. Everybody called him Sy. He came to the Palace one summer, found a job, and never left. That happened to lots of people. Sy lived in a noisy alley not far from the Forum of Constantine. He dealt blackjack and baccarat at the Palace and worked for Henry's father on the side because everybody said he was a genius and had a head for numbers. He wore granny glasses and read books and said things like, "I didn't choose this life, so I might as well make the worst of it." He was one of the nicest people Henry knew.

Henry's father made fun of Sy all the time. He called him a scrawny little nerd, which meant that he liked him and thought he was smart. Sy didn't just have a head for numbers; he was great with cards too and could do lots of different tricks. When they first met, Sy said he was putting together a floor show and looking for a manager, but Henry's father said, "Forget managers; you and me are gonna make a killing some day, and it won't be doing magic shows." Henry's father became good friends with Sy. So did the Whore of Jersey City, but nobody knew they were in trouble—or that Sy and Helena's mother were in love—until they all ran away together.

"Wait a minute," Father Crowley said. "Who ran away?"

Henry said we all did. Running away is what brought us together.

"I don't understand," the priest said and squinched up his face. Then he waved his hand. "But never mind. Go on."

Sy took Henry to the Hippodrome to watch the races all the time. He also taught him to read and write Greek and Latin and Hebrew and Aramaic and Coptic. Henry studied until late every night because he wanted to be an intellectual. Sy said intellectuals had to read and go to school for a long time. He said there weren't many of them around anymore and it was hard to become one because you had to spend years doing nothing and the cost of living had gotten out of hand. One time Sy took Henry to church. Not the Hagia Sophia but a church just like it in Pleasantville. He told Henry that going to church was sort of like finding a center in the universe. He knelt down and pulled Henry down next to him and took off his granny glasses and put his hands over his eyes and stayed that way for a long time. Henry got up and walked around the empty church and played with the candles until Sy was finished. "I don't want you telling anybody where we were," Sy said on the way back to the Palace.

Henry asked why.

"Because I don't want anybody to know, that's why."

Henry asked why not.

"Because I just don't. It's nobody's business."

Henry asked why not.

"Because I said so."

Henry asked why again.

"Let's just say I'm a catholic Jew."

Henry asked what that meant.

"It means I'm the opposite of a skeptic." He patted Henry on the knee and drove a little longer. "It means I believe in *everything*. And that means I can't belong to any one group."

Henry asked why not.

"Because that's the way it is."

Henry asked why it was that way.

"Because, by definition, all groups are exclusive. If you buy into one, it means you have to rule certain things out. I'd hate to rule something out and then find out later that I was *wrong*. Wouldn't you?"

Father Crowley leaned forward. His face was so close that Henry could smell his breath. It smelled bad—like the floor of the ice cream store. "Sy said all this to you?"

Henry nodded and the priest shook his head.

When they got back to the Palace, Sy took Henry to a place on the boardwalk to play pinball. "You have to keep the things you take seriously to yourself, Henry. That's the most important thing." They were playing a pinball game called Ace in the Hole. "It's important to keep a low profile. Even if you are certain about everything you know and are dying to shout it from the rooftops—you can't. Not unless you are willing to pay the price."

Henry asked what the price was.

"Well, for starters, most people will think you're an idiot. But even if you can get past that, the price is too steep. There's no way anyone can pay it and stay alive. Jesus Christ had to die on the cross in order to pay up! He was a catholic Jew too, and said he was the son of God."

Father Crowley sat on the sofa and pinched his eyes with his fingers while Henry talked and took books from the shelf and put them back. He looked at Henry for a long time. "Has anyone besides this Sy ever talked to you about God?"

Henry said God was only a name.

"You watch what you're saying, young man. Blasphemy is a very serious sin. I don't want any more of that talk. Do you understand?"

Henry asked to be taken back to the O'Briens'.

"We'll leave when I'm good and ready," the priest said.

Henry sat down. His sneakers had come untied.

"Tell me more about this Nike business," the priest said.

During the Nike riots Byzantium was almost completely destroyed by the Blues and the Greens. *Nike* means *victory* in Greek but that day when they went out on the beach, Henry's father didn't seem victorious. He was worried. Henry knew when his father was worried because he talked on the telephone a lot—not on his cell phone or the one in the suite or even one of the pay phones in the lobby. When Henry's father was worried he left the Palace to make his phone calls. Sometimes he went next door to Balley's Wild West and sometimes he walked way down the boardwalk and used one of the outside telephones. You couldn't be too careful. The emperor's agents and Theodora's spies were everywhere. Henry's father didn't want to take any chances. That's why he sent Henry and Helena and the Whore of Jersey City out of the city with Sy.

"We'll go back one day and it'll be like nothing happened," Sy said as they drove away in the car.

"You better be right," Helena's mother said. She twisted the rearview mirror so she could look into it and put on some lipstick.

"Things'll fall into place," Sy said.

"They goddamn well better," Helena's mother grumbled.

"Anyway, no point worrying about it now," Sy said. "What's done is done."

They went to Sy's sister's house in Philadelphia—not the Greek city but the one on the Delaware River. Henry's father came to Philadelphia the next day. He was driving the Maserati Quattroporte. It was the first time Henry ever saw the car. It was all black and had soft leather seats. Henry asked where he got it. "I won it," his father said. They went out for pizza, but Henry wasn't hungry.

"How come you aren't eating?" his father asked.

Henry said he didn't like anchovies.

"You don't like anchovies? Pizza without anchovies is like a dog without legs, kid." His father picked them off and piled them on his plate.

Henry wanted to know how long he would have to stay in Philadelphia.

His father called the waiter and asked for fresh-squeezed orange juice. "You want anything else to drink, Henry?"

Henry said no.

When the waiter came back his father looked into the glass. "What the hell is this? I asked for fresh-squeezed orange juice." The waiter took it back. "I've found a good school for you, kid. And a nice family to put you up too. Their name is O'Brien."

Henry said he didn't want to go to school or live with anyone called O'Brien.

"I don't want any arguments, kid. I know what's best." He took another slice of pizza. "Besides, it's not just my idea."

Henry wanted to know whose idea it was.

His father took another bite and wiped his mouth before answering. The pizza restaurant was filling up with families and was getting noisy. "Some social workers've been getting on my case. That's the long and short of it. If we don't do it my way, they'll take you and do it their way."

Henry asked what social workers were.

"It's a long story, kid. Don't worry. It'll all make sense to you someday."

Henry asked what day.

"The day you stop picking all the anchovies off your pizza," his father said and folded another slice in his hand and bit down and made a grunting noise.

Henry asked his father if he was growing a beard.

His father chewed and rubbed his cheek. "Thought I'd try out a new look. What do you think?"

Henry said it made him look different.

His father smiled and winked. "Thought maybe it would go with the car. Know what I mean? Hey, what about that chain I gave you?"

Henry showed him the chain. He wore it under his shirt.

"Don't lose it," his father said and took another bite of pizza.

After the restaurant they went for a drive. His father told Henry all about Maseratis and how it wasn't just any old car but a car with a great history behind it. "Ever since I was a kid I loved Maseratis. The year I was born was the year Fangio won the Argentine Grand Prix and the World Championship in a 250F. He was one of the greatest race car drivers ever. When I was your age I wanted to be just like Fangio."

It was bedtime when they got back to Sy's sister's house. Henry's father tucked him in and went downstairs. Henry snuck out of bed and tried to listen at the top of the stairs while the grown-ups talked, but they went into the kitchen and he couldn't hear. He went back to bed and dreamed he was Fangio driving the Maserati 250F that won the World Championship and the Argentine Grand Prix. In the morning when he woke up his father and Sy and Helena's mother were gone.

"Where'd they go?" Helena asked.

"All they said is they have some business," Sy's sister said.

Henry asked where his father was.

"Don't worry, honey," Sy's sister said. "You're staying here with me. They'll be back soon." Then she handed him a box. "He told me to give you this."

Henry opened the box. He didn't want a Gameboy. He didn't want any presents. He wanted to know where his father was.

Helena ran upstairs and locked herself into the bedroom.

Sy's sister took Henry into the kitchen. It was a mess from the night before. "Mind keeping me company while I straighten up a little?"

Henry asked where his father went.

Sy's sister bent down and put her hands on Henry's shoulders. "Don't worry, Henry. He'll be back soon. You and Helena are going to stay with me for a little while. We'll have fun together. I promise."

It was getting to be afternoon and Henry could hear people coming and going from the rectory. Father Crowley asked if he wanted to go outside in the yard for some fresh air but Henry shook his head and just kept talking. He told Father Crowley about Sy's sister's clothes store called Mitzi. Helena got to work there. Henry wasn't old enough to do anything useful so he went down the street to the library and read books. One book he especially liked was by Procopius called *Anecdota,* or *The Secret History.* That was how Henry learned all about Byzantium and the Emperor Justinian and his wife, Theodora. He also found some gnostic books that had been found in a cave in Egypt. They were very, very old. The books said how the whole universe was created and explained about how all the bad things came into it. Everything in the universe was all a big mistake. Henry read the books over and over every day until he knew them all by heart. When he was tired he slept in the back of the store.

Sometimes after closing the store they went to the health club. Sy's sister and Helena worked out in the gym and swam laps. Henry horsed around mostly and got yelled at once by an old man for slamming locker doors in the men's changing room. One time on the way home Sy's sister said, "I'd kill to have a body like yours, girl."

"Sometimes I think it's more of a pain in the ass than it's worth," Helena said.

He asked Helena if her body always ached. Helena laughed. "It's not *having* a good body, it's *keeping* it. That's what I meant."

This was how Henry learned about the corruption of the flesh.

"What did I just say about the language, Henry?" Father Crowley had his eyes closed to listen but now he opened them and gave Henry a stern look. He shook his head slowly back and forth and wagged his finger. Then he closed his eyes again so Henry could get on with the story.

After dinner when it was still too light to go to bed Sy's sister would bring the phone outside on the back steps and smoke cigarettes and call people. She said "innnnner-estingly enough" all the time. Henry played in the back yard that wasn't really a yard since it was mostly cement and used to be a driveway. There was a high fence and the gate was broken and the only thing holding it up was a rusty old chain. The key to the padlock was lost so you couldn't open the gate anymore. Sy's sister said it was more private that way. She told Henry he wasn't allowed in the alley but one time when she was out he climbed over the fence.

Sy's sister had a boyfriend. His name was Henry too and whenever he came over he said, "Hiya Henry, how's it hangin'?" Big Henry was really, really big. He was more than six feet four inches tall and wore size thirteen shoes. He lived in Chestnut Hill but kept his underwear and shoes and socks at Sy's sister's house because he liked to spend the night. He liked baseball too and was born in 1958, the year Mickey Mantle hit his five hundredth home run off Stu Miller to beat the Orioles six to five. Once he took Henry to the Hippodrome to see a Phillies game and bought him a pennant. Big Henry had season tickets, which meant he sat in the same seat at every game and was friends with everyone. He had four hot dogs, two bags of popcorn, and seven beers. "Great game, Henry. Right?"

Henry said he guessed so.

"You want to know why it was good?"

Henry said yes.

"Because Scott Rolen homered twice for the fifth time in his career, going three for three with three runs scored, and to top it all off we gave the Diamondbacks their eleventh loss in twelve games. That's why."

When they came home Sy's sister got mad. She said Big Henry was drunk. He went away mad and didn't come back for a long time. Sy's sister went around sad the next day and barely talked to anyone.

That happened right when Helena fell in love with Mohammed Ali—not the prophet or the boxer but one of the al-Samman clan in Egypt. He came into the store one day and when he left Helena said he was gorgeous. Mohammed Ali came in almost every day and bought something each time. Then one day he asked Helena to come to dinner with him and after that Helena started spending all her time with him.

Mohammed Ali was a businessman. He drove a Mercedes 450 SEL and traveled all over on business. Henry asked if he was a silk merchant but he only laughed. Henry told him it was good he wasn't a silk merchant because the secret of silk had already been brought back from China by two Nestorian monks. They gave it to Belisarius's wife. They even brought some worms with them and some mulberry bushes for the worms to eat. Belisarius made his wife pass the secret on to the emperor and empress and Procopius said Justinian and Theodora built a monastery for the monks in return. Then *they* took over the silk business.

Sy's sister said Mohammed Ali looked like Omar Sharif, but Helena said he was even more handsome than Omar Sharif. He smoked black cigarettes with golden tips that came from somewhere in the Caucasus. Sy's sister let him smoke in the store even though it wasn't allowed and when he offered her one she took it and lit up even though she never smoked except when she talked on the phone on the back steps. Mohammed Ali gave Helena lots of presents. He gave Henry a present too. It was a pure white Arabian stallion. But Henry had to give it back because he didn't have anyplace to keep it.

Helena started staying out all night with Mohammed Ali and one morning they came back and told Sy's sister they wanted to talk to her. They told Henry to go outside. Henry listened under the window and discovered that Mohammed Ali wanted Helena to come live with him.

"You're barely eighteen!" Sy's sister said.

"That's old enough," Helena said.

"I wouldn't be so sure of that."

"Why do you say that?" Mohammed Ali asked. "You don't think I can take care of her?"

Sy's sister didn't say anything.

"She will have everything she wants," Mohammed Ali said.

"At least wait until your mother gets back," Sy's sister said.

Mohammed Ali got mad. "Why do you insult me like this? I will not ask that woman for anything!"

"She's still her mother," Sy's sister said.

"She is no mother," Mohammed Ali shouted. "I tell you what she is."

"You don't have to raise your voice," Sy's sister said.

"Excuse me," Mohammed Ali said. "I apologize."

"It doesn't matter what she says. It's up to me to decide," Helena said.

"Don't worry," Mohammed Ali said. "I will take the full responsibility."

Then they all went into the kitchen to talk and Henry couldn't hear anymore.

After Mohammed Ali left, Sy's sister and Helena talked in the living room. "You need to think this over," Sy's sister said.

"Well, I'm in love with him. That's all that matters."

"I'm happy for you," Sy's sister said. "But I still think it's a good idea to think about it for a while. What about school?"

Helena got mad. "What about it?"

"You return in the fall, don't you?"

"Are you kidding? So she can brag that she's putting her kid through college?"

"Come on, don't say that."

"Why not? It's the truth! And I'm sick of hearing it. Besides, who needs school? He's taking me to Egypt."

"Egypt?"

"He has a place in Cairo and a place here. We'll go back and forth."

"It sounds exciting, Helena. Really it does. When I was your age I would have felt the same way you do."

"So why are you talking like I'm about to ruin my *life?*"

"Because I'm not your age anymore, and I've seen things like this before."

"Don't *say* that! What's wrong with you? Don't you understand? I love him, and he cares about me."

"I think you should wait. Give it a little more time."

Helena ran upstairs crying.

The next day Helena and Henry were in the back room of Sy's sister's store. Helena was putting labels on dresses and Henry was practicing writing Coptic on the empty boxes with a red marker. He asked her what happened to Sy and her mother.

"They ran away."

Henry asked why.

"Because they're crooks, that's why!"

Henry used to think people ran away because they were sad but in *The Coptic Gnostic Library* he read that you didn't run away, you fell away.

"What's that supposed to mean?"

Henry explained that you fell from the light into darkness, from knowing into not knowing. When you ran away it was impossible to tell which way you were going. If you were going into darkness or light. It meant you could never know if things were going to get better or worse.

26

"Where do you get all this crap, Henry?" she asked.

Henry told her about *The Coptic Gnostic Library*. Then he asked Helena if her mother and Sy ran away to get away from them and be in a better place.

"I hope they went to hell," Helena said.

Henry knew all about hell. One afternoon he was playing behind the store when he saw a chariot run over a dog. The chariot driver didn't stop but whipped his horses up and drove off. Henry went to look at the dog. It was just like all the other dogs that lived in the streets and alleys of Philadelphia. They were skinny and ate garbage and mostly were scared of people. The one that was hit was still only a puppy and the wheel had crushed its back leg. It was crying and shaking and trying to get up and Henry didn't know what to do.

An old man came over. "Kill it!"

Henry got scared.

"Put it out of its misery!" the old man said.

Henry looked at the dog again. It was howling and squealing. He still didn't know what to do. The old man spat on the ground. He didn't have any teeth and his spit was almost as red as the dog's blood. "How would you like to go through hell like that? Lay there all mangled up? What would you want?"

Henry said he'd want to get better.

"You can't get better," the old man said. "You can only get worse." He spat on the ground again. "Kill the goddamn thing."

So Henry picked up a big rock and dropped it right on the puppy's head.

This was how Henry learned that the world originated through a transgression.

"All right. That's enough." Father Crowley slapped his hands on his knees. "You've worn me out, son," he said. They got up to go back to the O'Briens'. When they were in the car Father Crowley said, "We need to have another talk. I have lots of questions—especially about Philadelphia and Sy's sister." He also told Henry to stop telling stories in school because it was disruptive. "I don't want to hear any more reports, okay? No more talk about gnosticism or any of those books you read in Philadelphia. Got that?"

Henry asked why.

"Because you're not old enough to understand them. You're way too far ahead of yourself, young man. You should put that remarkable brain to proper use. Forget the nonsense you've been reading and pay better attention in school."

Henry asked the priest why nobody believed in gnostic books.

The priest frowned and drummed his fingers on the steering wheel. Then his eyebrows went up and down and when he talked he stared straight ahead at the road and didn't look at Henry. "Because they are not the words of Jesus. They were written by men who wanted to create their own religion using whatever words and ideas they felt like.

They invented everything by mixing up whatever came into their heads with whatever pagan ideas they liked, and the only reason their books lasted is because some of them had been hidden in caves. They are not the true gospels. Period." He put his hand on Henry's knee and smiled. "Henry, you're a remarkable boy. I've never met anyone like you. But you'd better watch out that your gifts don't get you in trouble. God loves those who love the truth."

Henry wondered what difference it made to God or Father Crowley or anyone what books he read and what books existed. He wondered if any of the books of the Bible had ever been found in caves.

When they arrived back at the O'Briens', Mrs. O'Brien was standing at the front door. She came out to the car. She had curlers in her hair and walked like a big red duck. "Come in. Come in."

"I'd love to, Mrs. O'Brien, but I can't today. We had a good time together, didn't we, Henry?"

Henry nodded.

"If you don't mind, I'd like to come again next Saturday. Would that be okay with you?"

Mrs. O'Brien leaned into the driver's window. "He's not in trouble, is he, Father?"

"No. Not at all. He's a remarkable little boy. It's just— well, I can't describe it. His head is filled with ideas he's too young to understand."

"Don't I know it," Mrs. O'Brien said and waved good-bye.

When they were inside she yelled at Henry for being a troublemaker and whacked him on the back of the head and said she was going to call his father.

On Monday Henry had to go to the principal's office again. "Have you been behaving yourself, young man?" Sister Agnes Mary asked him.

Henry didn't say anything. He was scared of Sister Agnes Mary.

"I spoke with Mrs. O'Brien this morning," she said. "She tells me that you are still telling lies and stories."

Henry said Mrs. O'Brien was a liar.

Sister Agnes Mary grabbed him by the wrists. "If you ever speak like that again, you will be punished, young man. Do you understand me?" She gritted her teeth and Henry saw the spit fly from her lips. It reminded him of the old man in the alley. When she let go his wrists were red and sore. Henry cried and wished his father would come and take him back to the Palace. Gnostics didn't belong in Catholic school. In the Gospel of Phillip it said that they who inherited dead things are dead themselves. Words are dead things because they are all true. It was the same with stories. They were all true and that was why he liked to tell them. If everything is true one thing is no more true than another and all words will dissolve into their origins.

Henry decided to run away. He told Sister Agnes Mary he had to go to the bathroom. There was a window there and he opened the window and climbed out. When he was outside he ran to the bus stop. He had enough lunch money to buy a ticket and he got on the first bus that came. When he got on he sat in the last seat and tried to make himself as small as he could so nobody would see him. He remembered what he had read about running away. It was scary. He was alone on the open road. There were bad people on the highways—Tartars, Bulgarians, Goths, Huns, Cappadocians. People from all the corners of the empire. He didn't know where to go or what to do when he got there.

After a while he got off the bus and looked around. He was on a wide road—probably in Phrygia someplace. There was a 7-11 and a McDonald's. Their signs stood high up on narrow metal columns. Henry was glad to see them because they were familiar and there was comfort in signs that were firmly established. He hid in a dumpster behind 7-11 where it was neither dark nor light but only dim and where he hoped the archons would not get him. Archons are bad angels and there are lots of them. Athoth has a sheep's face, Eloaiou has a donkey's face, Astaphaios has a hyena's face, Yao has a serpent's face with seven heads, Sabaoth has a dragon's face, Adonin has a monkey's face, and Sabbede has a shining fire face. Henry got scared. Maybe he would have to wait for a long time before anybody found him. He would be like those scrolls that were in caves for so long nobody knew what they were when they were found. When they were put there they were one thing and when they were discovered they were the same

31

thing but the world was something else, like if you put a piece of meat in the oven and then burned down the house and then opened the oven and the meat was still raw.

There were magazines in the dumpster. They had pictures of naked men and women doing stuff to each other. Henry guessed it was fucking but even though people said *fuck* all the time, he wasn't sure it was like the pictures. He remembered one day when he was out on the beach with Helena and she talked to him about her mother. "She's an exhibitionist," Helena said. "All she wants is to be looked at all the time." She explained how her mother used to be in movies. "It's so embarrassing! If anyone at school ever found out about my mother, I'd have to leave."

Henry asked why.

"Because she used to be a porn star."

Henry asked what a porn star was.

"You know, pornography?"

Henry asked if it was like spirograph.

Helena laughed. "Right. It's just like spirograph."

They stopped talking for a little while. Then Helena asked, "Do you even know what a spirograph is?"

Henry said it was an instrument for recording breathing movements.

"Where'd you hear that?"

Henry said he read it in a book.

Helena dug her feet into the sand. "Well, it's a toy too. I used to have one."

Henry was digging a hole, scooping it out and piling

the sand around the edge to make a fort. Helena watched
and then after a while she said, "She isn't really a whore—
even though everybody calls her that."

Henry kept digging and when the hole was big
enough he told Helena to come into it with him. They
worked together making the walls higher and higher. "Has
anyone ever talked to you about sex?" Helena asked.

Henry didn't know what to say so he didn't say anything.

Helena was quiet for a while, then she said, "You can't
imagine what it's like to have these dumb men hanging
around my mother all the time."

Henry said he guessed not.

"Just because they saw her fucking in a movie, they
somehow think *they're* going to fuck her too. They're always surprised when it doesn't happen."

Henry said he guessed so and piled more sand onto a
collapsing wall. He asked Helena if her mother had ever
shot anyone.

"Are you listening to anything I've said?" Helena
asked.

Henry said yeah.

"If I think about it too much it drives me crazy."

Henry asked what drove her crazy.

Helena dug her foot into the wet sand and kicked a
blob of it onto the wall Henry was working to build up. "I
shouldn't be talking to you like this. You're too young."

Henry piled the sand faster and faster as a wave sent a

big lip of foaming water into one side of the fort, making the outside walls smooth. Helena kicked more wet sand onto the wall Henry was working on. "I've never seen any of the movies my mother was in," she said. "When I was twelve she told me about everything. She said she wasn't sorry for anything she'd done, and I shouldn't think that what she'd done was bad. She said she wanted me to know everything since one day I'd find out anyway. She offered to let me see one of the movies if I wanted, but she said she'd prefer it if I chose not to. You want to know how I see it all now?"

Henry said okay.

"I have this friend at school named Martha. Her dad was in the Vietnam War. Martha told me that as long as she could never imagine what he'd seen and done, it was okay. It's *normal* not to imagine your parents doing certain things."

Henry asked Helena if sex was fucking.

Helena got a surprised look. "I can't believe I'm talking to you like this." She didn't say anything for a while and began smoothing out one of the sand walls and patting it with her hand. Then her face got all red. "Forget what I said, Henry." They smoothed out the walls and patted them and some other kids came over and stood outside the fort and watched them. "It's time to go home," Helena said. "I'm getting sunburned."

Henry got out of the dumpster. The pictures made him wish he hadn't seen them. They showed people with

strange looks on their faces rubbing their hairy parts together. It reminded him of animals and was kind of sad.

It was dark and someone yelled, *"Hey!"* Henry ran
around to the front of 7-11 and went inside. He took out
all his money and counted it. It was more than five dollars.
The first thing was to call Sy's sister but when he tried to
remember her name all he could remember was the name
of the store and the joke she made about it: *If you wanna be
ritzy, you gotta shop Mitzi*. There was a pay phone outside the
7-11. He went back outside and got a plastic milk crate
and stood up on it so he could reach the phone. Then he
called the operator and said he wanted to call Mitzi in
Philadelphia collect but nobody answered at the shop and
Henry hung up.

One thing was sure. He wasn't in Byzantium anymore. Where he was now you needed a car and to have a
car you needed to have a license. In the good old days
Henry rode around in chariots and if he was lost there
were plenty of saints and angels around to talk to and
they'd always offer to get him back home if he needed it.
Saints were good to have around because they could see
through walls and around corners and they always knew
about all the killing and lying and cheating that was going
on everywhere they went. Angels were the same but they
could fly and see through people too. Not just through
their clothes but into their thoughts. Also, angels usually
dressed well and carried weapons. Saints went around
barefoot and sometimes even naked and were usually

filthy and broke because they always gave away everything they had. Nobody liked to talk to them. Angels and
saints both knew about the visible and the invisible and
the different things that couldn't be talked about and also
that God was a fuckup but that was why you had to love
Him. He had made a big mess of things. It was up to them
to try to help out. That's what they were there for. To help
straighten things out. Saints didn't mind being poor and
filthy and angels didn't mind flying around fixing things
all the time. Being an angel would have been okay. But
Henry didn't have any weapons or know how to fix stuff.
So he decided to become a saint.

He tried to call Sy's sister again but there was no answer. There was nothing he could do except not cry and
wait. He didn't want anybody to see him. Saints had to be
careful. When you were a saint people wanted stuff from
you and if you didn't give them what they wanted they'd try
to kill you. Lots of saints got killed by people who didn't get
what they wanted out of them.

Henry climbed back into the dumpster. It got cold and
Henry got even more hungry. Even though it was only the
end of September and there were still leaves on the trees it
felt like winter. Henry began to shiver. He wondered what
Mrs. O'Brien was thinking right now. She was probably glad
he was gone but mad because he'd left all his stuff at her
house. He could hear her going, "Lord, oh Lord," and fan-
ning the air with her hand. He could hear Mr. O'Brien
telling her to shut up in his sleepy voice. Henry started to

cry. He was about to go and give himself up when a cat jumped onto his lap and began purring and rubbing up against him. At first the cat scared him but then he remembered that saints could talk to animals. When you know that everything is in code you begin to understand the world.

In the morning Henry went around to the front of the store and called Sy's sister. This time she was there. "Henry! What a surprise! How are you?"

He told her he was at 7-11 and asked if she would come pick him up.

"Henry? Are you all right? Where are you?"

Henry said he waited all night until she came to the store because he didn't want to go to Catholic school or live with the O'Briens anymore. He wanted to live with her because he liked it in Philadelphia.

"Oh my god, Henry. You ran away?"

Henry said yes.

"Where are you? Do you know where you are? Go inside and ask somebody to come to the phone, Henry. Go find a grown-up for me to talk to."

Henry went inside and asked the man behind the counter with big tattoos on his arms to come outside. At first the man didn't say anything but then he went outside and talked to Sy's sister. When he was finished he gave the phone back to Henry. "Henry, you stay there, okay? Stay with the man I just talked to until somebody comes to get you. Do you understand? Henry? Are you all right? Oh my god. This is terrible. Henry? Are you there?"

Henry promised to stay put. He put the phone down and followed the man with the tattoos back inside. The man gave him a doughnut and some milk. "Someone will be here to get you real soon, kid," he said. "Don't run away on me, okay?"

Sy's sister never came. Henry was taken back to the O'Briens' house by two members of the imperial guards who put him in the back seat of their car and talked on the radio. One of the guards turned around. "What's your name, son?"

Henry was scared and didn't say anything.

"Don't worry, son. Everything's going to be all right. We're taking you back to your momma and daddy."

Henry shook his head and said no they weren't, they were taking him to the O'Briens'.

The guard raised his eyebrows.

Henry said I hid myself from them because of their wickedness, and they did not recognize me.

The guard looked at Henry for a minute and then he turned around and talked to the other guard, who was driving. After a little while he picked up the radio and talked into it but Henry couldn't keep his eyes open anymore and he fell asleep and didn't hear what was said.

He woke up a little while later, just as they were pulling up in front of the O'Briens' house. Mr. and Mrs. O'Brien and Father Crowley were all waiting on the doorstep. Mrs. O'Brien waddled down the walk and grabbed Henry and hugged him and said, "Lord, oh Lord," about fifty times, and, "Thank God you're safe."

Mr. O'Brien just said, "You shouldn't have done it, boy. You had us all pretty scared." He shook his tired head back and forth. They talked to the imperial guards for a few minutes. After that everybody went into the house and Mrs. O'Brien called Henry's father.

Henry didn't want to talk because everybody was watching him. "I'll come to see you as soon as I can, kid. Promise me you'll try to be good."

Henry asked if he was going to be punished.

"Don't worry. Nobody's going to punish you. Just try and be good. I'll get there as soon as I can."

Mrs. O'Brien and the imperial guard who had asked him his name and then the priest got on the phone and talked to Henry's father. Mr. O'Brien took Henry into the kitchen and made him a liverwurst sandwich.

The next Saturday Father Crowley came to get Henry again and this time he talked to Mrs. O'Brien for a while. They all went upstairs and the priest looked at every book Henry had in his room. "These books don't belong to you, Henry," he said. "They belong to the Philadelphia Public Library. They have to be returned." He said he was going to Philadelphia next week and he would return them but Henry would have to pay the fine.

Then they went to the rectory. There was no stopping for ice cream. They went straight into the same room as last time. The priest put Henry's books down on a table and sorted them into two piles. "Okay, Henry, what do you want to talk about?"

Henry said nothing.

"How about we talk some more about gnosticism?" The priest sat down on a chair in front of the fireplace and pinched the bridge of his nose. "First, let's get something straight. I don't want to hear any smart-aleck talk."

Henry said I'm not a smart aleck, Father, I am a saint.

11
NEW YORK CITY

It was Christmas vacation and Henry's father came to pick him up. He wasn't driving the Maserati Quattroporte but a Jaguar XJS. He brought presents for the O'Briens' and Mrs. O'Brien opened both of them even though one was for Mr. O'Brien. She put the book about hot-air balloons on the coffee table and the set of crystal ice cream dishes in the cabinet.

"How's everything going?" Henry's father asked.

Mrs. O'Brien said things were shaping up. "Slowly but surely. Father Crowley is very interested in Henry. They spend almost every Saturday together. Don't you, Henry?"

Henry didn't say anything.

"There are still problems at school, though." She looked at Henry with a fake look. "Isn't that right, Henry?"

Henry didn't say anything. He wanted to get going.

When they were in the car Henry's father sang, "Off we go into the wild blue yonder, flying high into the sun."

Henry asked what had happened to the Maserati.

"I traded it."

Henry asked why.

"It was time for a change."

Henry asked if Jaguars were better than Maseratis.

"Not better, just different."

Henry asked if Jaguars had a great history like Maseratis did.

"Not history, kid. Heritage. Jaguars have heritage." He patted Henry on the knee. Then he put on a cassette of Christmas songs. His father sang along with the music. He knew all the words. It was sunny and cold outside and they drove for a while just listening to the music and not talking. It was good to be with his father again.

Henry couldn't wait to see the Palace. Procopius said that after the Nike riots Theodora and the Emperor Justinian worked to rebuild the old sanctuaries and fortifications. They also built many new ones. The old wall of Constantine was a ruin. The city had expanded beyond it. Theodora and Justinian not only wanted Constantinople to have magnificent buildings, they also wanted to protect the city from invasion. The Hagia Sophia was destroyed by fire and the emperor hired Isidorus of Miletus and Anthemius of Tralles and ten thousand Isaurian workers to rebuild it. *Hagia Sophia* means *holy wisdom* and Henry wondered what wisdom there was in a big old church.

Henry looked at his father driving and singing and thought what belongs to him is mine. As long as the son himself is small he is not entrusted with his own. When he

becomes a man, his father gives him all things that belong
to him. He thought of Father Crowley. They called him
Father but whose father was he? He sang songs in church
and read things from the Old Testament and the Gospels
and the Acts of the Apostles and letters written by Paul,
who used to be Saul until he saw God and fell off his horse.
Sy once told Henry that Paul was one of his heroes because seeing God made him forget who he was and when
you had that kind of amnesia the world was a thrilling
place to be.

Henry opened up the glove box. It was filled with cas-
settes. He took them all out. His father looked at him and
patted him on the knee. "Put on whatever you want," he
said.

Henry was thinking about all the things he would do
when they got to the Palace. First he would see if
Theodora still swam in the mornings. He would sneak up
to the second-floor balcony overlooking the pool and wait
until she arrived. He had a dream one night that he dove
into the pool and swam behind her. She let him follow her
through the water down into its deepest depths. But in his
dream he somehow also never dove in because he was
scared of drowning. It was like that in dreams. You could
do one thing and also the exact opposite and both somehow seemed real.

Henry remembered the first time he saw Theodora up
close. She came to the Palace right after Henry and his father moved in. It was a long, long time ago and Henry

didn't really remember the old apartment near the Gate of Eugenius. He sort of remembered Ten Cents a Dance, a woman who lived with them when Henry was little. Henry's father called her that because she was a dancer at the Taj Mahal. She came from Bulimia and was nice at first but then she got mean. After she moved out Henry and his father moved into the Palace. Right after that Theodora came. Henry knew about her before she arrived because he heard everybody talking. Henry's father called her a pain-in-the-ass MBA type and said they were all going to have to learn to deal with her. He also said it was a good thing she was drop-dead gorgeous because she was going to need all the help she could get running the place.

One day Henry was playing in the men's bathroom near the aqueduct of Valens. The aqueduct brought water into the city over the hills. He had just turned on all the faucets and was about to run away and hide when a big gray-haired man came in. Henry slipped into the janitor's closet. It wasn't the emperor but a man Henry's father called the Big Cheese. Sy said he was head of restructuring. He'd been at the Palace for two days. Henry followed him out of the bathroom and down to the slot machines. Kids weren't allowed so he waited outside in the lobby and counted the chariots and the horses and the lepers and the beggars who were always hanging around waiting for their luck to change.

After a long time the man came through the lobby with Theodora. When she saw Henry she beckoned him over. "We even have our very own Eloise," she said to the gray-haired man and put her hand on Henry's shoulder. The man looked at Henry and didn't say anything. Henry was scared. He thought he was caught for turning on all the faucets. The man just looked at Henry and then nodded and they continued on. Henry followed them outside and watched the man get into a limo and drive away.

Henry asked his father why Theodora had called him Eloise.

"It was a joke," his father said.

Henry said he *wasn't* Eloise.

"We're lucky she didn't call you history, kid."

Henry asked what Eloise meant.

"It means she's gonna let you stay is what it means."

Henry asked why.

"It's some kid book about a kid who lives in a big hotel. The first thing she said to me was that you reminded her of it. Good thing too."

Henry asked why.

They were having breakfast on the balcony and his father was wearing the boxer's robe he always wore in the morning. It said TYSON on the back and was made of pure silk and he had gotten it at a famous fight way back in the olden days. Henry's father said it was one of the all-time great fights and he'd won a big bundle on it. He tapped his fingers on the table and took a sip of orange juice and pulled the belt of his TYSON robe. Then he said, "Because it means she's got a soft spot underneath that hard ass of hers."

Henry couldn't wait to get back to the Palace. He would watch the games and spend a day at the Hippodrome—even if Sy wasn't there to take him. He would make a circuit of the gates. He would start at the apartment near the Gate of Eugenius. He would bless all the hotels and casinos and public baths and churches, for now he was Henry of Atlantic City, and every city needed a patron saint.

Henry asked his father when they would be at the Palace.

"We're not going to the Palace, kid."

Henry asked where they were going.

"I'm taking you to the Big Apple."

Henry asked where the Big Apple was.

"We'll be there in about an hour, kid. We're going to have a great time together. Just you and me."

Henry had heard about the Big Apple. It was a city. Sy had told Henry about it one day at the Hippodrome. They were in the stands looking down at the track and waiting for the race to start. "It's like life in the big city, Henry," Sy said. "The fastest horse wins." Henry asked which big city and Sy said he was talking about the Big Apple. Henry asked Sy if he'd ever been there. "I used to live there," Sy said. Then he started yelling and screaming because the horses had begun to race. That's the way it was in the Hippodrome. The horses ran and ran and ran while the people watched and screamed. Henry's father stopped going to the Hippodrome when he became captain of the Blues. Before that he went almost every day.

Sy liked to bet. "It's part of my religion," he said. "It proves that God made the world but does not intervene in his creation afterward."

Henry asked what that meant.

"Take a look around." Sy gave Henry his binoculars.

Henry looked down at the track but the race hadn't started yet and there wasn't anything to see.

"No! Look here." He pointed to all the people in the stands.

Henry still didn't get it, so after a few minutes he gave Sy the binoculars and asked if he could have a Coke.

"The reason God doesn't interfere in his creation is because it's against his rules," Sy said. "Everybody who bets on a horse prays to God that it will win, right?"

Henry said he didn't know.

"Sure they do. But think about it. If God answered all those prayers, then *all* horses would have to win! And that's impossible, right?"

Henry said he didn't know.

"Believe me, Henry. It is. So the way I figure it is, if God doesn't influence outcomes, it means he can't answer any prayers, right? I mean, a deity has to be consistent, right?"

Henry didn't say anything.

"That must mean that God is estranged from his own creation. *Deus absconditus.* That's the theological term. And it's a good thing too."

Henry asked why.

"Because it's how *odds* came into existence, dummy."

Henry asked Sy what odds were.

"Use your noodle, kid. You want me to explain everything?"

Henry said yes.

"Okay, odds are chances, and chances are the degree to which people believe that God will *not* change his own rules in the middle of the race and interfere in the outcome. Got that? Sure, anything is *possible*, but some things are more likely to happen than others, right? God *can't* answer prayers—and that's what makes people free to bet!"

Henry asked Sy why he prayed that time when they went to the Hagia Sophia.

"I'm glad you asked that," Sy said. "Most people who don't know any better ask God to do things for them. But that's not praying. That's just wishful thinking. When you pray you don't ask God to do things for *you*. You ask yourself to do things for *God*. Since he can't answer prayers, I figure he needs all the help he can get."

Henry asked what kind of things Sy could do for God.

"Things that are hard, things a *Deus absconditus* could never do for you."

Henry asked what things.

"Controlling your passions, for one. That's what free will is all about. Personally, I kind of like the idea that the world will have to be destroyed so that it can be saved. But I figure it's *Homo absconditus* who is going to do all the dirty work."

Henry asked who *Homo absconditus* was.

Sy poked his finger into Henry's chest. "You and me, kid." Then he laughed out loud in a funny way and looked down at the racing horses through the binoculars.

Henry asked Sy what passions were.

Sy watched the horses through the binoculars. "Passions? They're the things you always want too much of."

Henry said like what.

Sy shouted, "GO! GO! GO!" and pressed the binoculars into his eye sockets. Then he slapped his thigh and said, "Like winning, goddamnit. Winning! Winning! Winning!"

Sy's horse lost the race but they stayed for two more anyway and his horses lost those races too. He swore and tore up his tickets and tossed them in the air. "I am alpha, I am omega, the beginning of all things and their end," he said.

Henry asked what that meant.

"It means that God is a cosmic fuckup! And one day this whole mess is going to have to be cleared away."

Back then Henry thought Sy was just mad because he'd lost so much money. Now he understood a little better. Sometimes it had seemed as if Sy was only talking to himself, and it didn't matter if Henry or anyone else was listening. But then he would get a funny look and say, "Right? Know what I mean?" as if Henry were the only person in the world Sy would ever say such things to. One time he told Henry saints and angels didn't have passions because they didn't want anything. They were allowed to interfere

in God's creation because they weren't trying to *get* anything out of it. Saints and angels could have great power
over people and that was also how they could go astray.
That's why there were good angels and bad ones. Sy said
Napoleon and Hitler and Mussolini and Big Fingers Johnny
were bad angels, and when God made people free to bet he
also made bad angels by accident. But just because he made
them by accident, it didn't mean he could change any of his
rules. It was written that those that have gone astray whom
the spirit begets go astray also through him.

Henry asked his father how fast Jaguars could go.

His father stepped on the gas until the car was going
super, *super* fast. "We're gonna have a good time, kid," he
said and put on some more music.

They went to a big hotel across from a park. Henry's father
said it was the most famous hotel in the city and he let a
man drive the Jaguar away. The hotel was sort of like the
Palace except there weren't any slot machines. They went
up to their room and Henry's father said in the Big Apple
you lived large. He told Henry they had a busy schedule
and to get cleaned up and rested while he made some
phone calls. Henry asked if there was a library.

"Are you kidding? The best library in the world is just
down the street! But what do you want at the library, kid?
We have a ton of things to do!"

Henry said he wanted to get some books.

"No problem! The best bookstore in the world is just down the street. You want books? We'll go get books. It's Christmas, kid. You can have anything you want."

When Henry was taking his nap an angel appeared to him. But instead of appearing to him in a tongue of flame or holding a sword, it entered his ear and stayed there. It told him that the children of the heavenly man were more numerous than those of the earthly man. It said that the children of the heavenly man had once been on the earth. They had passed through the degradation of the life of the flesh.

Henry asked the angel what the degradation of the life of the flesh was and the angel said it was everything necessary to keep the body alive. It was everything that passed from the mouth through the entrails and out of the body.

Henry asked if the angel was talking about shit.

The angel said no, it meant the body, which turned everything that passed through it into shit.

When he woke up from his nap, Henry's father told him they were going out to see Sy and Jersey City .

Henry said he thought they ran away.

"Where'd you get that idea from?"

Henry said Helena and Sy's sister.

"We're meeting them for dinner, kid. How could we be meeting them for dinner if they ran away?" He handed Henry a big red shopping bag. "I got you some new clothes. Go see if they fit."

Henry went to his room and put on the new clothes.

He looked in the mirror. He didn't want to wear them because saints weren't supposed to wear new things, especially fancy new things. But they weren't supposed to complain either. As Henry got dressed the angel in his ear said that in this world those who put on garments are more precious than the garments.

"How do the shoes fit?" his father asked in the elevator. Henry said fine.

"You look like a million bucks, kid," his father said and jabbed him in the stomach.

Sy and the Whore of Jersey City were waiting inside the restaurant. Henry didn't recognize them at first because Sy had a beard and wasn't wearing glasses and looked fat and Helena's mother had black hair instead of blond hair frizzed out and was wearing round granny glasses like Sy used to wear. They made her look old.

"Well, well, well. Look who's here." Sy smiled when he saw Henry.

Henry asked where Helena was.

Helena's mother got a funny look on her face and didn't say anything.

"She's got a boyfriend," Sy said.

"Some goddamn Egyptian playboy," Jersey City said. "The son of a bitch." She began to cry. Henry had never seen her cry before. Her mouth and her eyes didn't seem connected. Sy gave her the napkin from his lap. "The bastard won't even let her come to the phone."

"Maybe she doesn't want to," Henry's father said.

"I'm her mother, for Christ's sake. I feel like calling the cops."

"Very funny."

"She's barely eighteen!"

Henry's father patted Jersey City on the arm. "Take it easy. Things'll be all right. She's a little pissed off, that's all. Give it some time. She'll come around."

"No, she won't. I know she won't. Everything's all fucked up. A complete mess."

Henry's father leaned forward and took Jersey City's hand but she jerked it away and put her napkin to her eyes and started crying again. Her hands shook and Henry noticed that they were wrinkled and the skin was chapped. "It's all fucked up," Helena's mother said again. "Look at me! I'm afraid to even look in the mirror."

"Don't sweat it, kid," Henry's father said. "Pretty soon everything will be back to normal. Now just stay put. I'm arranging a meeting."

"Look," Sy said, "I don't want to go to any meetings. I just want to get the hell out of here."

"Take it easy, Sy. Don't do this to me. All right? I'm putting some finishing touches on things."

"What kind of finishing touches?"

"Trust me. The main thing now is to stick with the program!"

"You're insane. I can't believe I'm tied up in this."

"You're not tied up in it, Sy. You're up to your ass in it. Now, sit tight and wait."

"I feel like one of those witness protection people."

"Well, there ain't no witnesses and you don't need protection, so just stop the whining, will you?"

The waiter came to take their order.

Henry said he didn't want to eat.

"You have to eat, kid. You haven't eaten all day."

Henry said he was fasting.

"Veal parmigiana for the comedian here," his father said and the waiter wrote it down.

"So, Henry, tell me about school," Sy said.

Henry said it was all right.

"Had a few little problems, but things are looking up," Henry's father said.

"What kind of problems?" Sy asked.

Henry said theological ones.

Sy laughed. "I know what you mean, kid."

Henry said no he didn't.

"Stop being a wiseass," his father said.

"He's not being a wiseass," Sy said. "He's being Henry. We understand each other, don't we, kid? Remember our talks?"

Henry said he remembered them but it looked like Sy had forgotten them.

Henry's father clipped him on the back of the head. "If you don't stop the wisecracks, you'll spend the rest of this vacation in the hotel room."

When the waiter brought the veal parmigiana Henry said he couldn't eat it.

"Eat it," his father said. "You order, you eat."

Henry said he didn't order it.

"Don't get wise, kid. Just eat it."

Henry said food was shit.

Henry's father grabbed him by the arm and hoisted him out of his chair and led him to the men's room. He picked him up and sat him down on the edge of the sink. "Look, I'm not going to tolerate any more big-mouth stuff. You got that? If you don't cut it out you'll find yourself back at the O'Briens' by tomorrow morning. Understand?"

Henry didn't say anything.

His father stared straight into his eyes. Henry stared straight back. Then his father turned away and put his hands in his pockets. "You think I'm being mean? I'm just trying to do what's right, Henry. I'm sorry if you're mad at me for leaving you at the O'Briens'. But we don't have too many options, kid. That's the long and short of it. Life's full of tough lessons. Believe me, I know it more than most. And I know you have it tough too, but you don't have it *that* tough. I'm doing the best I can, kid. Believe me. You don't know what tough is." He put his hand on Henry's shoulder. "This is a vacation. Let's call a truce, okay?" They shook hands. "Nice chain! Where'd you get it?"

Henry said you gave it to me.

"Don't you forget it either." Then he lifted him down from the sink. "Let's try to have a little fun, okay?" They went back to the table, where Jersey City was still crying. Her eyes and her napkin were all black from mascara.

"Christ," Henry's father said. "I've never been around so many miserable bastards in my life! What did you think? That everything would just fall into your lap? What's the matter with you? Stop thinking about how miserable you are, and let's get the job done." Everybody ate and nobody said anything for a long time. "Instead of whining about how scared you are, think about what you'll do with all the money," he said when they were almost finished eating. "Have a little faith, for Christ's sake."

"It's hard to have faith when you're in the dark about everything," Sy said.

Then Jersey City said, "Mind if we change the subject?"

"I'd love nothing more than to change the subject."

"Sy and me are married."

Henry's father looked up and then dropped his knife and fork onto his plate. "You're what? Married? Is that true, Sy?"

"We were going to keep it a secret until it was all over," Sy said.

"Of all the goddamned things! Why keep it a secret?" He dropped his napkin and ordered a bottle of champagne. After the waiter poured the champagne Henry's father lifted up his glass. "May your life together be happy." Then he took a sip. "It goddamn well better be." He laughed in a way that Henry had never heard him laugh before and clapped Sy on the shoulder. "Goddamn, Sy! You're one smart bastard, you know that? I gotta hand it to you. It never would have occurred to me to *marry* her for the extra cut."

"Fuck you," Jersey City said. "I wouldn't marry you if you were the last man on earth."

After that everybody was happy again.

When they were back in the hotel, the angel in Henry's ear told Henry to go to the window and look outside. Henry pulled the curtains back and looked out the window. The angel asked Henry what he saw.

Henry said tall buildings and a park and cars moving on the street below.

The angel said the city was the manifestation of creatures that eat of the body. The city comes into being. It devours itself and the creatures that dwell within it devour each other. It said the earthly city was a defilement of the heavenly city.

Henry asked the angel what else there was to see.

The angel said knowledge of what is hidden.

Henry asked the angel how he could know something that was hidden.

The angel said the one who has come to knowledge is also called the one who knows himself.

Henry asked the angel how you could know yourself.

The angel said by not being taken captive by a sweetness of darkness and carried off in a fragrant pleasure.

Henry wanted to ask if all darkness was sweet but the angel went away.

In the morning Henry looked out the window again. It was snowing. The streets were filled with slush when Henry and his father went outside. Henry's father said it was too wet to walk so they got a taxi. He said it was time to get some Christmas shopping done. "I'm taking you to one of the best places in the world. Ever hear of F. A. O. Schwartz?"

Henry said no.

When they were inside the store Henry's father said, "Okay, kid, where to?"

Henry said he didn't know.

"You like games?"

Henry said he guessed so.

They went into a row that was filled with games. Henry's father took down different things and asked Henry if he thought they looked interesting. Henry didn't know what he wanted. Then they walked around some more. "Do you like to build models? When I was a kid I was crazy about models."

Henry said he'd never built a model.

"Model building is a fine art. Some models are so good you'd almost swear they were real. Once, when I was a kid, I built a model of the *Titanic*. It was so real—you know what? I wanted to sink it as soon as it was finished!"

His father took down boxes with pictures of battleships and airplanes on them but Henry said he didn't really feel like building models. They walked through the store and stopped in front of a gigantic train set. His father took his hand and said, "Pretty amazing, huh?" Henry nodded. It was the most beautiful little world he had ever seen.

"Incredible, isn't it?" his father said.

Henry nodded again. He was about to ask if maybe he could have one when his father ruffled his hair and said, "Too bad it's not for sale. When I was your age I wanted one exactly like it. But it's only a display. They put it out every Christmas. It's one of a kind."

Henry wished that he could shrink himself down to the size of the little toy engineer and drive the train through the tunnels and around the snow-covered mountains and stop at the little toy towns where the houses had lights shining in the windows and everybody looked like they were at home. Henry wondered if his angel could see what he was seeing; then he realized that to an angel, the whole world probably looked like a toy train set and suddenly he was scared. They watched the trains until his father said, "C'mon Henry. There's tons of other stuff to see." They went to another part of the store that had video games. It was loud. Henry looked around at all the games but nothing was as good as the train set and that made him feel sad. He wondered how many children there were in the world and if some of them got everything they wanted or if they all deserved everything they got.

He asked his father if they could leave.

"I don't believe it. You want to go?"

Henry nodded.

"You don't want to get anything?"

Henry said no.

"You still mad about last night?"

Henry shook his head.

"Then why do you want to go?"

Henry said he just did.

They went outside. Henry's father said they were only a few blocks from a gigantic bookstore. He asked if Henry wanted to go.

Henry said okay.

"I didn't realize you were such an intellectual, kid. What are they teaching you at that school?"

Henry said nothing.

The bookstore was almost as big as F. A. O. Schwartz. Henry looked and looked but he couldn't find the books he used to have.

"Exactly what sorts of books are you looking for?" his father asked.

Henry said he had to go to the library to get them.

"Jesus Christ, Henry. What are you reading?"

Henry said *The Secret History* by Procopius and *The Coptic Gnostic Library*.

"What the hell are they?"

Henry said *The Secret History* was about Justinian and Theodora and the gnostic books were found in a cave in Egypt.

"I'll be goddamned, you really are some sort of genius, aren't you? What's the word? Prodigal? Something like that." He took a book called *Invertebrate Biology* from the shelf. "How about some science? This is pretty heavy stuff."

Henry said no thanks.

"Okay then, Einstein, let's go."

They went to a big building with two huge lions outside. "This is the New York Public Library, kid. If you can't get it here, it don't exist."

It was the biggest library Henry had ever seen. Inside were statues and marble floors. The reading room was huge. It was the biggest room Henry had ever seen that wasn't filled with slot machines. And it was quiet.

They went to the information desk. "Tell them what you want," Henry's father said.

"Have you checked the card catalog?" a man with a mustache asked.

Henry shook his head.

"Do you know what it is you are looking for?"

"Some secret history and some books that came from a cave in Egypt," Henry's father said.

The man reached for some papers and rolled his eyes.

"Look, just help the kid find them," Henry's father said.

"I am here to help locate books, not to do people's research for them."

Henry's father grabbed the man's wrist. "Then locate the boy some books, buddy."

The man yanked back his hand. "I will call a security guard if you don't leave the building immediately."

"Don't threaten me, you little faggot."

A woman came over and asked what was going on.

"My son needs help finding some books."

"I'm sorry, but you'll have to leave," the woman said.

"Look. He just wants to look at some books, all right?"

"This is a research library, sir. We do not circulate books. You can go to a branch library if you want to take out books."

Just then a security guard came up. "Okay, let's go."

They went back to the hotel because Henry's father said he had to get changed for a meeting. In the taxi he told Henry that he was on his own again tonight but that tomorrow was Christmas Eve and they had some more visiting to do.

Sy had left a message at the hotel. Henry's father called him as soon as they got to the room. He got mad and yelled into the telephone. "You let her go? What the fuck is wrong with you?"

Sy said something.

"What good does that do me? If I only needed you I would have said I only needed you. I should never have let you out of my sight!"

Sy said something.

"I don't care if she was *pissing* bricks! I said I needed both of you!"

Sy said something.

"I don't know, goddamnit. Listen to me, you stupid son of a bitch! You get your ass over here right now."

Sy said something.

"I don't care. I'm not letting you out of my sight."

Sy said something.

"No. Leave it. You can go back for it later. Just get your ass over here. You're staying with me. And hey, Henry's alone here. Bring some movies or something."

Sy said something.

"Fine." He slammed the phone down. "Stupid god-damn bitch!" He went into the bathroom and took a shower. When he got out he ordered freshly squeezed orange juice from room service and asked if Henry wanted anything.

Henry said he wanted orange juice too.

"Speaking of orange juice, does Mrs. O'Brien give you vitamins to take?"

Henry said no.

"I want you to start. Remind me. You need vitamins. Make a new man out of you."

Henry said the cup of prayer contains wine and water and it is full of the Holy Spirit and belongs to the wholly perfect man.

Henry's father put on his belt and shook his head.

"Whatever you say, kid." He went into the bedroom to get a jacket.

When Sy came Henry's father yelled at him and asked what was the matter with him? Sy started to say something but Henry's father wouldn't let him talk. "I don't want to hear it."

"It's probably better not to have her around anyway."

"Godamnit, I'm the one who decides who's going to be around and who isn't. Where'd she go, anyway?"

"Back to Mexico. Look, I tried to stop her, okay? She was hysterical."

"Fucking useless crybabies." Henry's father was standing at the door. He put on sunglasses and held out his arms. "So, do I look like De Niro or what?"

"Yeah, mucho dinero."

Henry's father pinched Sy's cheek. Then he jabbed his finger into Sy's chest. "Don't fuck with me anymore, Sy. Don't you fuck with me." Then he left.

"How about a movie, Henry?"

Henry said okay.

Sy opened the bag he had brought and took out some videos.

Henry asked Sy if he knew who Father Crowley was. "Who?"

Henry said Father Crowley was a Catholic priest.

"I don't know any priests. I don't know any rabbis either, come to think of it. Or ministers or brahmins or monks."

Henry said Father Crowley had told him that there were only four gospels and none of them had been found in caves.

"That's because Father Crowley is a Catholic with a big C, and that's what big-C Catholics believe." Sy went to the window and pulled the curtain shut, then went to turn on the TV. "If you're *really* catholic, though, you never rule *anything* out." Sy took a piece of chocolate out of his pocket and broke it in half and offered some to Henry. "Are we going to watch a movie, or are we going to have a theological discussion?"

Henry said he didn't care. But what he would like would be to get those books.

"What books?"

Henry said the ones he found in the library next to Sy's sister's store, *The Secret History* and *The Coptic Gnostic Library*.

Sy laughed. "Oh, *those* books."

Henry said it is impossible that anyone see anything of those things which are firmly established unless he becomes like them.

"Go on."

Henry said unlike the case of man who is in the world, he sees the sun but is not the sun and sees the heaven and the earth and all the other things but he is not these.

"Nice. Very nice. Go on, go on."

Henry said it is not so with the truth because he sees the truth and is the truth.

"Somebody needs to write a book about *you!* If I wasn't stuck in this mess, I'd do it myself."

Henry said only the wretched labor in vain.

"Right you are, kid. Anyway. We're sort of stuck here for now."

Somehow, Sy had changed. He was like someone who went down into the water and came up with nothing. In Byzantium Sy was different. There he was like someone who went down into the water and came up with a fish but let the fish go afterward. Maybe he went down too many times. Maybe he let go of a fish he should have kept. Or maybe he kept a fish he should have let go.

Henry remembered one day when he had gone with Helena to Sy's place. There was a big box in the middle of the room and Sy said it was an orgone accumulator and he built it himself. He said the box captured all the energy in the universe and concentrated it inside and if you sat in the box you could feel the energy. It was called *orgone*. Henry wanted to go inside but Sy said no. He said you had to be prepared.

Helena laughed at Sy and said he was crazy. Sy had a book that was written by a man named Wilhelm Reich, who had invented the box and gone to prison because, Sy said, he had discovered a new level of human consciousness the same way Jesus Christ had. Sy said Reich called Christ the archetypal genital character. He said he had followed the instructions for the orgone accumulator very carefully and every day he sat in it for a little while.

Helena asked what he did inside.

"I work toward my full orgastic capacity."

"That's disgusting," Helena said.

"I'm talking about orgone energy," Sy said. "The living pulse of the universe."

Sy took more chocolate out of his pocket and ate some and gave a piece to Henry. Then he took out the video and put it in the VCR.

Henry asked what the movie was.

"*Total Recall*. With Arnold Schwarzenegger."

Henry said he had never heard of it.

"I'm not surprised," Sy said and gave Henry another piece of chocolate. Sy sat on the couch and Henry lay down on the floor and they watched the movie. Afterward Sy asked Henry if he liked it.

Henry said it was all wrong.

"How can a movie be all wrong?"

Henry said because Schwarzenegger was not nailed to a tree in the end and the world was saved anyway. In the divided world there are those who come to know the truth and those who despise the truth because they are created by error. Error created this world and that was why Jesus had to come and ransom it back for his father by getting killed.

"Jesus, Henry," Sy said.

Henry said the only lost causes are the ones who can't rise above ignorance and see that the world they live in is a void of darkness and drunkenness and sleep and illusion.

"Maybe you should take a break from that stuff you've been reading."

Henry asked why.

"Because one day you might wake up and find out that all the things you've been saying are, well, true. Like what the guy said to Schwarzenegger when he's in the Recall Office picking out his fantasy trip. You remember the line?"

Henry said you get the girl, kill all the bad guys, and save the entire planet?

"No, before that."

Henry said you dumb bitch, he's just acting out the secret-agent part of his ego trip?

"No, before that."

Henry said when you go Recall you get nothing but first-class memories?

"No."

Henry said when you travel with Recall everything is perfect?

"Right after that."

Henry said take a vacation from yourself?

"That's it! Take a vacation from yourself. I like that. It's taken me thirty-nine years to figure that one out." He ruffled Henry's hair with his hand.

Henry said his favorite line in the movie was I wanted him dead, you moron, or I wouldn't have dumped him down on Earth.

"I liked that one too. Anyway, enough movie talk. I'm hungry. What are you in the mood for?"

Henry said nothing.

"That won't do, kid. What do you say we get a little room service?" Room service delivered a whole table of food and Sy ate everything and drank three bottles of beer. Henry didn't eat anything but watched Sy as he gobbled everything up. He had been transformed from a lover of truth into a lover of food. Henry asked Sy to take him to the library.

"We'll do it in the morning."

Henry's father came back a little while later. He unbuttoned his shirt and sat on the couch and put his feet up on the table. He looked like a bear. "You two have fun?" he asked. "What movie'd you watch?"

"*Total Recall*. Henry's a tough critic," Sy said.

"Oh yeah?"

"Henry wanted to see Schwarzenegger nailed to a tree in the end."

Henry's father laughed and pulled Henry over onto his lap. "I don't blame you, kid. I get sick of the good guys always winning in the end too." Then he said it was time for bed.

Henry didn't go to sleep but stood at the door and listened while Sy and his father talked.

"You telling me they *bought* it?" Sy was saying. "They actually *believed* you? Christ almighty. Now they have *both* our asses in a sling!"

"Trust me, Sy. It all makes perfect sense. The story is air-fucking-tight. I've been over it with the old man ten times already. Tomorrow you'll see for yourself. Just wait. Oh, and he wants me to bring Henry too."

"What? Henry? What the hell for?"

"Beats me. Some kind of assurance, maybe."

"Assurance? For what?"

"Fuck if I know. He's known about Henry from the beginning. He's got a soft spot for kids. Maybe he wants to see what kind of a family man I am. Who the hell knows?"

"I don't believe this. You can't be serious. Henry's only a kid, for Christ's sake. You can't mix him up in this."

"I got news for you, Sy. He's already mixed up in it. Anyway, when he sees all that money we'll both be golden."

"We're bringing the money with us?"

"Goddamn right. A Christmas present."

"And what if he doesn't like how much is there?"

"Jesus Christ! How many times do I have to explain it? I'm not going to say it again. Just wait'll he sees the green stuff. When we hand over the cash, everything will fit in just perfectly."

"So you told him she was padding the numbers?"

"One thing at a time, buddy. One thing at a time."

Henry went to the bed and lay down. He tried to forget himself and Byzantium and the Big Apple and everything but he couldn't. He went to the window and looked out into the darkness of Central Park. His angel said those who have come to know themselves will enjoy their possessions.

Henry asked the angel what happened if you had nothing to possess. He had his face pressed to the glass of the window, trying to look down at the street below.

The angel said then the light will descend upon you and you will be clothed in it.

Henry tried to imagine being clothed in the light but he couldn't. He was disappointed. It was like that sometimes between divided egos and lovers of the truth.

There was an owl in the emperor's garden. It lived in a tree. One of the guards had the job of finding mice for it to eat. The mouse got left in the grass somewhere on the big lawn. After a while the owl swooped down and grabbed it and took it back up into the tree to eat. Life in the emperor's garden was easy. There was a wall around it and a long, long driveway that went through some woods. There were statues and fountains and terraced gardens and springs with flowing water and gazebos. There was even a helicopter landing pad with a big red X painted across it and a swimming pool.

"Looks like fucking East Egg," Sy said.

"Don't be so nervous," Henry's father said as they drove up to the gate.

"Don't be nervous? How can I *not* be nervous?"

A guard at the gate stopped them and talked into his walkie-talkie before letting them through. They drove slowly through the grounds until another guard stepped out from nowhere and pointed to where they should park the car. They got out of the car and Henry's father opened the trunk and pulled out a big suitcase. As they walked toward the house he asked Henry if he still had the gold chain. When Henry showed it, his father put down the suitcase and picked him up and kissed him on both cheeks.

Procopius said the emperor rarely ever left the Palace grounds except to go to the Hippodrome. He was always surrounded by people. They came from all parts of the empire and grew so numerous after the wars with Persia and Carthage that he ordered a special hostel built in the Palace for them to stay in. Henry had only seen the emperor once before. It was a long time ago during the Easter festival in the Forum of Constantine, where Henry and his father were supervising the slaughter of the Paschal Lambs. Justinian and Theodora were generous at Easter. They provided lambs to be roasted for all the people of Byzantium. Not just a few but thousands and not just in the Forum of Constantine but in all the public areas throughout the city. As captain of the Blues Henry's father helped keep order during the festival. Just as the big charcoal fires over which the lamb would be cooked were being lit, Justinian entered the Forum with Belisarius, who had just returned from the war with Persia. At first nobody noticed because they were not dressed in their normal regalia or accompanied by the regular guard. They just rode into the Forum of Constantine on their horses as if they were ordinary people. It was noisy and the air was thick with smoke from the fires and everybody was watching the soldiers do the slaughtering. Henry figured it was what battle looked like. There was blood everywhere and a strong smell of viscera. The two men rode through the crowd and when somebody shouted, "Hail Justinian, emperor of Rome," and someone else shouted, "Hail Belisarius, commander of the armies," a cheering began that drowned out even the bleating of the doomed animals. The people pressed around the two men on all sides and the emperor and his general made their way slowly until they reached the big pit where the meat was being cooked and then one of the Blues gave them each a leg of roasted lamb. Belisarius ate his but the emperor refused because he always fasted at Easter and took nothing but water and bitter herbs for three days. They sat on their horses and watched the festival while the people cheered them. Then a detachment of the Palace guard made its way through the crowd and surrounded them and made the people stand back. That was before the Nike riots, when the Hagia Sophia was burned down, and before Belisarius was publicly disgraced and made to walk the streets of Byzantium as a beggar and when the emperor was not afraid of the people.

They followed the guard down a long corridor lined with statues. Some statues were missing arms and some were missing heads and one was missing completely. The pedestal had a little card on it. The emperor was a great lover of antiquity.

"You behave yourself, kid," Henry's father said.

The emperor was sitting behind a big desk and was surrounded by his generals. They all looked up when Henry and his father and Sy entered the room. Henry was surprised because they were all old men and the room smelled kind of sour, like old men. The emperor motioned for everybody to be seated. He beckoned Henry to come to him. Henry walked around behind the desk and the emperor leaned forward in his chair and whispered into Henry's ear. "Do you love your father?" he asked. He turned his head so Henry could answer.

Henry whispered into the emperor's ear who is he that exists except the Father alone?

The emperor looked across his desk at the room full of men and smiled. Then he picked Henry up and sat him on his knee. He was much stronger than he looked. He swiveled in his chair so their backs were to the men in the room and they were looking out the window over the beach. The waves crashed silently in the distance and outside it was cold and gray December. The emperor stroked the back of Henry's head. "Tell me, son. Should I believe what your father has come here to tell me? Is he telling the truth?" One of the generals sneezed and blew his nose. Without turning around Henry knew it was Sittas the Thracian because he had a cold he could never get rid of. He had caught it in the mountains when he was trying to persuade the Armenians to leave their mountain homes and become part of the empire.

Henry cupped both his hands over the emperor's shaggy ear and said if we know the truth, we shall find the fruits of the truth in us; if we unite with it, it will bring our fulfillment.

The emperor was quiet for a long time and kept stroking the back of Henry's head. The generals were getting restless. Then the emperor whispered in Henry's ear, "What do you want to be when you grow up?"

Henry cupped both hands over the emperor's ear again and said a saint.

The emperor laughed and then he lifted Henry off his lap and told him to go sit down. Then he swiveled around so he was facing the men in the room. "Okay, gentlemen. What have you brought me?"

Germanus leaned forward in his chair. "How about the whole story?" he said in a low voice. Germanus had married an Anicii. The Aniciis came to Byzantium from Rome after it was conquered by the Ostrogoths. They were about as old and noble as families that could still call themselves Romans got and Theodora hated Germanus and his wife because they were aristocratic and rich whereas she had once been an actress who took off her clothes on stage and people knew what she looked like naked. Everybody knew that Theodora hated them only because she was jealous and they were never welcome in the Palace, which suited them just fine because they hated being anywhere near the rabble. People called Germanus the Grand Seigneur because he dressed in fancy clothes and spoke in a fancy way and had estates and palaces all over the empire.

"There's not much to say," Sy said slowly. "Except that I was asked to carry some money out of the country."

"What were your exact instructions?" Germanus asked.

"To deposit the cash and return with the deposit slip."

"Which bank?"

"ICCB. The International Commerce and Credit Bank."

"Did you ask why?"

"No."

"Did you have any idea yourself?"

"I assumed it was a tax thing."

"A tax thing," Germanus said. "What were you offered for helping out with this tax thing?"

"Two percent."

"And what did that come to?" Germanus asked.

"A little over sixty thousand dollars."

"So the total sum of the deposit would have been a little over three million?"

"That's correct," Sy said.

Germanus didn't look satisfied with Sy's answers and clasped his hands together with his fingers pointing up and put them to his lips like he was trying to wedge something between his front teeth.

"That's a nice little fee for taking a trip to the Bahamas," Solomon said. Solomon had been Belisarius's chief of staff in the Carthage expedition where the Arian Vandals were defeated and Gelimer, their king, was brought back to Byzantium in chains and made to walk in procession through the streets of the city. As he walked he looked around him and said, "O vanity of vanities, all is vanity," and when he reached the imperial box in the Hippodrome he was forced to prostrate himself before Justinian and Theodora. Solomon was from Daras in Mesopotamia and had a high, squeaky voice because he was a eunuch. He said it had happened in battle but everybody else said it had happened in a brothel in Tyre when he was asleep. The woman who did it to him was angry because he refused to take her back to Byzantium with him. As punishment she had her breasts cut off and the joke among the soldiers was a ball for a tit but anyone caught telling it had his head cut off, which gave rise to even more jokes.

"What made you change your mind and bring us the money instead?" Solomon asked.

"I didn't change my mind," Sy said. "I was told there was going to be a change of plan."

"Oh? You mean someone told you that you weren't *really* going to steal three million dollars after all? Is that it?"

"I wasn't told anything. I was just doing what I was told."

"Did you have any ideas about what you were involved in?"

"Yes."

"And what did you think it was?"

"Embezzlement."

Germanus lifted his fingers away from his lips. "We understand that. The question is by whom."

"I didn't want to know about it. I was just doing what I was told."

"You weren't even curious?" Solomon asked.

"No. I figured that kind of stuff was par for the course."

"Par for the course?" Solomon asked. "You telling me you think embezzlement is par for the course?"

"Let's just say that once I was asked, it never occurred to me to say no."

"Why not?" Germanus asked.

"Because I figured once I was asked, no was not an option." He smiled in a funny way, as if to say he'd made a joke. But nobody laughed. "It wasn't until the airport when everything got explained to me that I realized I was in deep shit. And I then I *really* knew I didn't have any options."

"Mind explaining that?"

"Look, there I am waiting in the airport with a suitcase full of cash, okay? And suddenly here comes the chief of security and tells me I can cooperate with him or I can kiss my ass good-bye. Those were the exact words. I thought I was dead meat."

"So you went along with him?"

"Of course I went along with him," Sy said. "What else was I supposed to do?"

John Troglita cleared his throat and spoke for the first time. "You say he caught up to you at the airport?"

"Half an hour before my flight."

John Troglita was also called John the Troglite. He was famous for his bad temper and was a specialist in search-and-destroy missions and punitive expeditions. The emperor had sent him to Africa to clean up after Belisarius's victory. He had carried out the emperor's orders by depopulating the place. Some people said he was insane but everyone agreed he was a great military man and there was even a long poem about him written by a Carthaginian schoolmaster that nobody read anymore.

"So at the airport you just decided to drop everything and follow this new plan. That was it?" John the Troglite asked.

"That's right."

"He told you that you were helping to lay a trap?"

"Yes."

"Describe the trap."

"It seemed pretty straightforward. Instead of taking the money out of the country, we would bring it directly to you. The story back at the Palace would be that I had stolen it. We'd give her time to doctor the books, then the money would be returned and she'd be exposed."

Henry's father stood up and put the suitcase down on the emperor's desk and turned it around and flipped it open so the emperor could see what was inside.

"Why should we believe a goddamn thing you're telling us?" John the Troglite asked.

Sy was quiet for a minute. "Maybe you shouldn't," he

finally said. "I'm sure there's a lot more going on here than I could ever know about."

"He's right about that," Henry's father said. "Mind if I talk now?"

John the Troglite nodded.

"The numbers were cooked from the start—in case he *did* run. Either way, she figured she'd be covered." He spread his arms. "A million here, a million there? What's the difference, right? Either he does what he's told and she's got a little offshore account set up for herself. Or he runs, takes the heat, and the cooked books cover her for the difference. Not a bad little scheme, huh?"

John the Troglite got mad and shouted at Henry's father: "Listen to me, you son of a bitch, I'm not asking you what *she* expected. The books say there's seven million dollars missing! Seven! I want to know why you only brought us three. Where's the rest of the money?"

Henry's father didn't look at John the Troglite; he looked at the emperor. "The books were cooked, sir. She had them cooked. It was part of the plan. I swear upon the soul of my mother and my mother's mother what you have there is everything." He looked at John the Troglite. "I am an honorable man and have acted out of loyalty to you."

John the Troglite was red in the face and about to start screaming again but the emperor held up his hand.

Henry's father looked around at all the men in the room. "It's all there. You have my final word."

Germanus unclasped his hands. "It's all a little too goddamn convenient," he said. Then he crossed his arms over his chest and looked at the emperor and shook his head. "As far as I'm concerned we ought to get rid of the whole stinking bunch." He waved his arm like he was sending something back to the kitchen.

John the Troglite agreed.

The emperor was quiet. Then after a few minutes he told Henry's father to stand up. "What punishment would you recommend?"

Henry's father looked around at the generals and at Sy. He looked everyone in the eye, proud and tough. "It's not for me to say."

"If you can make accusations, you can suggest punishments. Go ahead. You have my permission."

Henry's father looked at the ground for a minute, then looked up and smiled. "Give me her job."

The emperor drummed his fingers on the desk and then raised his hand and slapped it down hard. "I'm too tired to listen to any more." He beckoned to Sy.

Sy's face turned pale and he didn't get up from his chair.

The emperor beckoned to him again.

Sy rose and walked up and stood at the emperor's desk.

"I hear that you got married recently."

Sy nodded but didn't say anything.

The emperor opened up the suitcase. "Marriage is a sacred institution, and it sickens me to see it falling into ruin. Do you plan to have children?"

Sy nodded again and put one hand on the edge of the desk for support.

"Children are a great treasure," the emperor said and handed Sy three stacks of bills from the suitcase. "Thank you for the trust you've repaid me."

"I can't accept it, sir," Sy said.

"Take it," the emperor said. "Tomorrow is Christmas. Go and celebrate."

Then the emperor looked at Henry's father. "I will consider your request," he said. "You will have my decision after New Year's day." Henry's father held out his hand but the emperor didn't shake it. Instead he beckoned to Henry and took him on his knee. He stroked the back of Henry's head and said, "Don't worry, son. Don't you worry about a thing. And don't forget what you heard here today. One day you will understand and everything will make sense." Then he put Henry down and told everybody to leave.

Henry went back to the car with his father and Sy. One of the guards escorted them. Nobody said anything for a long time and Henry's father kept looking in the mirror while he drove. "What did the old man ask you?" he asked after they had gone a long way.

He asked if he should believe you, Henry said.

"What did you tell him?"

Henry said the truth, I told him to believe the truth.

Henry's father looked over his shoulder. "You are one amazing little bastard, you know that?" And he started laughing. Then Sy started to laugh too and Henry watched from the back seat while the two of them laughed so hard that Henry's father almost drove into the other lane. Sy said, "You're a fucking genius, Henry. And your old man has balls the size of the People's Republic of China!" Then after they had stopped laughing and had driven for a while longer Sy said, "Think he's going to give you the job?"

Henry's father didn't answer right away.

"Seems pretty likely, doesn't it?"

"I don't want to think about it," Henry's father said and kept on driving.

Back in the city they went to a bookstore where Sy said Henry would be able to get everything he wanted. The bookstore was filled from the floor to the ceiling with shelves and ladders to climb up on.

"Get whatever you want, kid," Sy said. "It's on me."

When Henry began to climb the ladders, the man who owned the shop came out from behind the desk. He talked with a stutter. "Excuse muh-muh-muh-me, gentle-men," he said. "This isn't a children's buh-buh-bookstore."

"My son isn't a normal child," Henry's father said.

"I'm sorry to hear that. This isn't a nuh-nuh-nuh-normal bookstore either." He motioned for Henry to come down. "Tell me what you want and I'll guh-guh-guh-get it for you."

Henry pointed to the top shelf.

"Henry's an authority on the gnostics," Sy said.

Henry could tell the owner was mad by the way he climbed up the ladder. When he was at the top he didn't turn around. "Okay. Which one do you wuh-wuh-want?"

Henry pointed to *The Coptic Gnostic Library* in the middle of the shelf.

"Are you sure?"

Henry nodded.

"It's a cuh-cuh-complete scholarly edition. You have to take them all."

"Fine. Bring them down," Sy said.

"Are you sure? The cuh-cuh-cuh-cost is seven hundred dollars."

"I just said we'll take them."

The owner reached out for the books one by one and started to climb down. "It's a complete set. You under-sta-sta-sta-stand. I can't break it up."

"No problem."

When the owner got down he looked at Henry and at Sy and Henry's father. "He's also interested in Procopius," Sy said.

"I only have the Loeb Library edition. It's complete but used."

"Fine."

The owner went away and came back with more books. They were exactly like the ones Henry had in Philadelphia. "Will that be all?"

"No," Sy said.

The owner looked half cranky, half sad. "What else can I do for you?"

"We'll take the whole shelf," Sy said, pointing up to the top shelf.

The owner looked at Henry and at Sy. "Is this suh-suh-some kind of practical joke? If it is, I'm nuh-nuh-not in the mood."

"We're not in the mood for jokes either," Henry's father said. "You want to sell the books or not?"

The bookstore owner didn't say anything else after that. He took all the books from the shelf and packed them into boxes. He took the money Sy gave him and counted it and put it in the drawer. Then he held the door open while they carried the boxes out and put them in the trunk of a taxi.

"This is where I vamoose," Sy said.

"Get in touch the usual way. But wait until after New Year's," Henry's father said.

Sy picked Henry up and hugged him and said, "I want to hear all about what's in those books." Then he got into a taxi. That was the last time Henry ever saw him.

On Christmas day Henry and his father walked in the park and then went to the ice-skating rink at Rockefeller Center. Henry's father was a good skater. He taught Henry how to go fast and stop and even how to go backward. He said going backward was the best way to meet girls. They skated around the ring a few more times and Henry asked his father if his mother was dead.

His father didn't answer. He put his hands behind his back. "C'mon. Watch how I do this. Can you skate like this? With your hands behind your back?" After they skated for a while he said, "Listen, Henry. Don't worry about your mother. Try not to think about it too much. Hey, how'd you like to go and see a hockey game?"

Henry asked his father again if his mother was dead.

"Yeah," his father said. "She's dead."

Henry asked how she died.

His father pulled him to the side and they stood there for a few minutes watching people skate past them. "I figured I had a few more years before the questions came," he said. "She died of an overdose."

Henry asked what an overdose was.

"You're too young for this, kid. I'll explain it all some other day."

Henry asked what his mother looked like.

His father pointed to a woman across the rink who was watching the ice skaters. "There! That's what your mother looked like."

Henry looked at the woman. Her hair was tucked up under a beret and she was standing with her hands in the pockets of a long overcoat. Then his father grabbed his hand and pulled him back onto the ice before he could see her features. By the time they got to the other side of the rink she was gone.

Henry asked his father what his mother was like and where she was buried.

"All I can say is your mother was the most beautiful woman in the world. If she were with us now everything would be different."

Henry asked where she was buried but his father said, "Stop. I don't like talking about it. Stop asking so many questions."

Henry said in the days when Eve was in Adam there was no death. When she separated from him death arose.

"Look, Henry. Quit talking like that, okay? It gives me the creeps." His father crossed his arms and they watched the other ice skaters for a little while. "I'm not the best father in the world. I know that, okay? But I'm doing the best I can. One day maybe you'll understand." Then he started skating again and Henry could see that he was frowning and his eyes were filled with tears and it wasn't from the cold wind.

That night the angel entered Henry's ear again and told him not to be deceived. The angel said the truth is like ignorance because while it is hidden it rests within itself. Henry got out of bed and went to the window. He watched the city consuming itself in a shower of lighted windows and he wondered what had happened in the world that brought people into it and left them to be in it all alone. He wondered how people whose mothers *weren't* dead were different, and why his father never wanted to talk about her.

He tried to open the window but it wasn't the opening kind, so he pressed his face against the glass so he could see all the way down to the street. He thought and thought as hard as he could and tried to remember the tiniest thing he could of the woman who had been his mother. But he couldn't get further back than the apartment near the Gate of Eugenius and Ten Cents a Dance. Was *she* his mother? If she was, then why hadn't she taken Henry with her when she left? If she was, then how did his father know she was dead? Why did his father get sad when Henry asked questions? No. Ten Cents a Dance could not have been his mother. Even if she was, she couldn't have been. She had left him behind and had only ever made his father angry. And Henry knew his father was sad. His father had always been sad.

Henry asked the angel who his mother was and the angel told him that all those who have fallen from the light and into the darkness of the body are born from a mother. Henry went back to bed and lay down and pulled the covers up over his head. He woke up a little while later. It was still dark. Henry didn't cry. He could hear his father snoring. He lay in bed and called on his angel and the angel whispered back. It said that the next-best thing to virgin birth was not to know your mother.

The next day Henry's father dropped him back at the O'Briens'. He carried all the boxes of books up to Henry's room, then talked to Mr. and Mrs. O'Brien for a little while. He gave Mrs. O'Brien a big envelope. She put it into a drawer next to the sink.

"Okay, kid. I guess this is it," his father said. He lifted Henry up in his arms and held him.

Henry asked when he was going to come back again.

"As soon as I can, kid. Just as soon as I can. You be good, now." He put Henry down and messed up his hair. "You still have that chain?" he asked.

Henry nodded.

"Remember who gave it to you," his father said and frowned the same way he had at the ice-skating rink. Henry followed him to the door. His father walked out to the street and got into the Jaguar without looking back. Henry stood in the door and watched his father drive away. He didn't wave and Henry didn't either.

A little while later Mrs. O'Brien came up into Henry's room. "Where'd you get these books?" She picked one up and held it in her hand, then put it down like it weighed too much.

From Sy, Henry told her.

"You know you're not supposed to be reading these things," she said.

Henry said they were his Christmas presents.

She stood in the door to Henry's room and put her hands into the smock she always wore when she cleaned the house. "I'm calling Father Crowley," she said. "If he says you can keep them, then it's all right by me." Henry lay on his bed and closed his eyes. A little while later he woke up and heard the priest and Mrs. O'Brien talking downstairs. Henry waited in his room. After a little while Father Crowley came in. "Merry Christmas, Henry." His eyes went straight to the books all around Henry's bed. "Did you have a nice time with your father?"

Henry said yes.

"Mind if I take a look at your new books?"

Henry said they're mine.

"I don't doubt it. Don't worry. I'm only curious." He sat on the bed and took each one and read the title out loud and put it down on the bed next to him. "Someone has spent a lot of money to provide all this reading material." He held up a book and said, "Sheer nonsense."

Henry asked why.

"Well, for one, there are no secret sayings of Jesus Christ. Jesus didn't keep secrets, Henry. Everything he said comes to us in the Holy Gospels written by Matthew, Mark, Luke, and John. The things you have here are historical curiosities. Not the truth of Christ."

Henry said while the truth is hidden it rests within itself.

"Would you mind explaining that?"

Henry said the truth is in itself so it can be contained in many vessels.

"But that does not mean every vessel contains the truth. Some vessels contain *false truths*. That kind of truth is evil."

Henry said there was no false truth because the truth contained itself and falsehood contained itself and falsehood could not be contained in truth.

The priest got up. "I guess it's going to take some more time before we understand each other. I want you to come to the rectory tomorrow to meet a friend of mine. Would you like that?"

Henry didn't want to go to the rectory to meet Father Crowley's friend. He wanted to go back to Philadelphia to live with Sy's sister.

They went downstairs and Mrs. O'Brien gave them Christmas cake to eat. "The cake is delicious," Father Crowley said.

"She bakes a mean cake," Mr. O'Brien said. He had crumbs in the corner of his mouth.

"Christmas is my favorite time for baking. And this is my favorite recipe." Mrs. O'Brien gave the priest another piece of cake. "You'd better eat it, Father. Else it'll go stale." Then she cut another piece for Mr. O'Brien, who always sat quietly and ate whatever was put in front of him. When he was finished he always said it was time to lie down.

"I'd like to come for Henry in the morning," Father Crowley said. "If you don't mind."

"Come as early as you like, Father. I'll have him ready when you get here."

The priest finished the cake and stood up and thanked Mrs. O'Brien and put on his coat and said good-bye. Henry went upstairs to his room and watched the priest get into his black Chevrolet Malibu and drive away.

That night before going to sleep Henry called on his angel to come save him. It was very late and everybody was asleep. Henry got out of bed and tiptoed downstairs into the kitchen. He opened the drawer next to the sink and took out the envelope his father had given Mrs. O'Brien. It was filled with hundred-dollar bills. Henry took some and put the envelope back and went back upstairs to bed. He dreamed about Arnold Schwarzenegger. He was wearing necklaces and was wrapped in a white sheet that was stained with blood. He had something to tell Henry but he couldn't get it out. Henry entered a huge church that was like the Hagia Sophia except that the outside was painted with designs and inside it was dark and smoky and a man was hanging from the ceiling upside down. His skin was all leathery and his hair was matted and he held his hands folded on his chest. Henry called up to the man and asked him if he was praying and the man said he was doing penance. Henry left the church and wandered through the woods and came upon big cities with churches in them and in each church somebody was doing penance.

Father Crowley came and got Henry in the morning. When they were in the car the priest said, "I need to pay a quick visit to a friend who is in the hospital, Henry. Maybe you can help me cheer her up a little."

Henry watched out the window and counted the buses on the street. In Byzantium if you needed perfume you went to the Augusteaum. If you wanted bronze work you went to the Mese. If you wanted horses you went to Amastrianum Square. If you wanted to talk to God or any of his angels and saints you went to the Hagia Sophia. Henry felt in his pocket for his money and wondered where you went if you wanted a cab.

"I went for a walk before morning mass," the priest said. "Sunrise is always more brilliant on cold mornings. Have you ever gotten up early to watch the sun rise?"

Henry said when you create something and it turns out well and beautiful you can be proud of your creation. But if your creation turns against you because of some flaw it is useless to try to find the fault somewhere else. The fault is not in the creation, it is with the creator.

Father Crowley didn't say anything and kept driving. Then he said, "It's going to be an interesting day, Henry. My friend is a priest and also a psychologist."

Henry asked what a psychologist was.

"A psychologist is someone who studies what happens in people's minds. Sometimes people talk to psychologists to try to understand what they are thinking and feeling."

Henry asked if that meant psychologists had fore-knowledge of the Perfect Mind.

"Would you mind explaining what you mean by that?"

Henry said *ennoia* was the Greek word for thought. It was Ennoia who came forth from the mind of the Father of the All and that's how the creation was started.

"Interesting. Which book did that come out of, Henry?"

Henry said it was from *The Apocryphon of John*.

"Try reading the *real* John, Henry. The Gospel of John says, *At the beginning of time the Word already was; and God had the Word abiding with him and the Word was God.* Dr. Alt will be interested in hearing what you have to say. I'm sure he knows all about *The Apocryphon of John.*"

Henry asked again if psychologists had foreknowledge of the Perfect Mind.

"I wouldn't know what to say, Henry. It's quite possible."

Henry said Ennoia performed a deed and Barbelo came forth and appeared before him in the shine of his light, the first power that came forth from his mind, the Pronoia of the All.

"Comic books, that's all it is. You might as well be reading comic books. You have an amazing gift, Henry. It's a gift from God. I only wish you were able to give some thought to what it is you are saying."

Henry said the world was created when God thought the first thought, which was the thought of Himself.

The priest turned into the driveway of the hospital and parked the car. He turned off the engine and sat for a minute. Then he said, "I suppose you could put it like that, Henry. It's a very nice way of putting it, as a matter of fact. But where does it lead you?"

Henry said it was selfish to think of yourself first and that's where God made the first mistake and plunged the world into creation. But the priest didn't hear him because he had already gotten out of the car. "Come along, Henry."

In the hospital Father Crowley said, "Mrs. Fontane is a very old woman and very ill. I want you to be polite and respectful."

"Good morning, Father, I hope you're not here to give me the last rites," Mrs. Fontane said when they entered the room.

Father Crowley smiled. "Good morning. Good morning." Then he introduced Henry.

"Come closer," the old lady said. Henry stood next to the bed. Mrs. Fontane touched his cheek with her hand. "Now, are you one of Laura's?"

"No, Mrs. Fontane. Henry's a new pupil at the school. We're going to spend the day together."

Mrs. Fontane's eyes were milky and blue and her hair was almost all gone and she was propped up on big pillows that made her look small. There was a bottle hanging upside down with a tube going into the back of one of her hands. She took some teeth out of a glass that was next to her bed and put them into her mouth but they didn't make her look any better.

"I'm glad to see that you're feeling more comfortable."

"I'm as comfortable as someone about to croak can be," Mrs. Fontane said.

"You certainly seem in fine spirits."

"Has my lawyer contacted you yet?"

"We're scheduled to meet next week."

"It's about time," Mrs. Fontane said. "What's taking him so long?"

"As far as I can tell, everything is in good order."

"It damn well better be," she said and looked at Henry. "Young man, if you ever want to become rich you had better become a priest or a lawyer. They're the ones who really know how to take advantage of old ladies. Right, Father?"

"It's usually doctors at the top of the list, Mrs. Fontane."

Mrs. Fontane made a wheezing noise and wiped her chin with her hand. "Well, I'm at their mercy too. But at least I can understand what they're talking about a little better."

"That's generous."

"Doctors are like libertines. They're only aroused by extreme circumstances."

Father Crowley picked up a fat book that was on her bedside table. A surprised look came over his face. "Mrs. Fontane!"

"Are you shocked, Father?"

Father Crowley fanned the pages of the book with his thumb. It was called *One Hundred and Twenty Days of Sodom*. "Yes. I am. I don't—I don't know what to say."

"Then don't say anything, Father. I always wanted to read the Marquis de Sade. I wish I had read it earlier. Have you read it?"

"I certainly haven't! It's pure pornography."

"You could call it that, Father. But you'd only be missing the point." She coughed into her hand. "I find it extremely entertaining, Father." She giggled in an old-lady way. "De Sade is a riot."

FREDERICK REUSS

The priest picked up the book again and opened it and read a page. "I wish you wouldn't say that, Mrs. Fontane. In my opinion this is sinful."

"Now, now, Father, what's so sinful about an old woman amusing herself on her deathbed? De Sade is really very harmless. And very, very imaginative." She tried to laugh but began to cough and a nurse came in.

"I'm afraid we have to leave," Father Crowley said. "Would you like to say a prayer?"

The old lady nodded and the priest took her hand and bowed his head and they said a short prayer together. When they were finished the nurse adjusted Mrs. Fontane on her pillows and asked if she would like some juice.

"Do you really think it's a sin, Father?" She smiled and her teeth slipped.

"I do. Yes. And I can't imagine why you would want to read such trash."

"The marquis says that Nature, despite all her disorder, is often sublime, even at her most depraved," Mrs. Fontane said. "Come back tomorrow. If I'm still alive we can talk about that."

"I don't have to wait until tomorrow. I'll tell you right now that I see nothing depraved about Nature."

Mrs. Fontane lifted both her arms with all the plastic tubing and held them up in front of her like two bent twigs. "Oh no, Father?" she said.

The priest put a hand on her forehead and made the sign of the cross. Mrs. Fontane closed her eyes and Henry could see her eyelids twitching. Then the priest blessed himself and said, "In the name of the Father, the Son, and the Holy Spirit, amen."

Henry was standing near the foot of Mrs. Fontane's bed and said no one will hide a large valuable object in something large, but many a time one has tossed countless thousands into something worth a penny.

"What was that, young man?" Mrs. Fontane tried to lift her head from her pillow. She gestured for him to come around to the side of the bed. "What did you mean by that?"

Henry said compare the soul, it is a precious thing and it came to be in a contemptible body.

Father Crowley took Henry's hand and pulled him away from the bed. "Don't take it personally, Mrs. Fontane. Henry is a—well, let's say he's special." Then he tried to lead Henry away.

"Wait. Let him be, Father."

The priest let go.

"I've just read that there is nothing more delicious than meting out punishments. I can't think of my condition as anything but a punishment." She looked sad.Nobody said anything. "For the life of me, I just can't understand it."

"The Lord often asks us to accept that which we cannot understand. Perhaps the Book of Job would be more appropriate reading now. I'm sorry. But it really is time for us to go." He took Henry's hand again.

"Hold on a moment, Father," she said and began to

read: *"In that nothing was more delicious than meting out punishments, in that nothing prepared the way for so many pleasures . . ."*

"Please, Mrs. Fontane, we *really* have to go."

Mrs. Fontane put the book aside. "The idea that punishment and pleasure can be linked! Father, do you think it is possible that God is enjoying all this?"

"Mrs. Fontane, please. I'd be happy to talk with you some other time. Now is really not appropriate."

Henry said the world came about through a mistake. For he who created it wanted to create it imperishable and immortal. He fell short of attaining his desire.

"That's quite enough." Father Crowley led Henry toward the door.

Mrs. Fontane closed her eyes. "Good-bye, Father." Then she opened her eyes. "Good-bye to you, young man, and thank you for coming."

"I'll come again tomorrow—with some books that might interest you."

"Save your books, Father. Piety is the worst disease of the soul."

The priest ushered Henry out of the room and they left the hospital. Father Crowley didn't say anything the whole way except that Mrs. Fontane was very old and very, very ill.

Dr. Alt arrived at the rectory just as Father Crowley and Henry were getting out of the car. He parked his car next to Father Crowley's and when he got out Father Crowley went up to him and they shook hands and talked for a minute in quiet voices. Then Father Crowley touched Dr. Alt on the elbow and the two walked over to where Henry was sitting on the steps. Dr. Alt walked with a cane.

"Henry, this is Dr. Alt."

Dr. Alt held out his hand and Henry shook it. "I'm pleased to meet you, Henry." He was much older than Father Crowley, with big glasses and bushy eyebrows. He also had an accent and was either an Ostrogoth or a Visigoth or a Vandal but Henry didn't know which one for sure. When he walked he leaned over his cane and he wore the same black suit and collar as Father Crowley except instead of polished black shoes he wore white running shoes. He didn't look like someone who had foreknowledge of the Perfect Mind.

Father Crowley led them into the sitting room. "I'll be right back," he said.

"Take your time," Dr. Alt said. There was a fire in the fireplace and a plate of cookies on the table. The old doctor sat down in a chair by the fire and took off his glasses and began to clean them with a handkerchief.

Henry looked at the bookshelves to see if there was anything new but it all looked like the same stuff and he took a cookie and then put it back because he didn't want to fall for any tricks.

Dr. Alt put his glasses back on and then blew his nose on the handkerchief. "Well now, Henry. Father Crowley tells me you have an interest in gnosticism."

Henry looked at the fire and didn't say anything.

"Maybe we have something in common. Tell me, Henry. How did you come to such an unusual—hobby?"

Henry said he didn't know and just then Father Crowley came into the room and asked if he could join them.

"Of course. Please. We are just getting started." Then Dr. Alt asked Henry to tell him how he had heard about the gnostics.

Henry said from *The Coptic Gnostic Library*.

The doctor stared at Henry from under his bushy eyebrows. Father Crowley got up from where he was sitting and began to walk around the room with his hands behind his back. Henry looked back at the old man and tried to see through him but all he could see was a swirl of leathery wrinkles and a bushy gray mustache and a faint light in his eyes that glowed like numina. He asked the priest if he had any money.

"Why do you ask?"

"Henry likes playing games," Father Crowley said.

The doctor leaned over and reached into his pocket and took out an old leather change purse and opened it and fished around for a coin. Finally he took out a quarter and gave it to Henry between pinched fingers. "Think of it as a token of friendship," he said.

Henry said he would do that and rubbed the quarter on his pants until it shone.

"Could you tell me about the books you've been reading?"

Henry said he had lots of books.

"Do you know the titles?"

Henry said he had all the books of Procopius and also *The Coptic Gnostic Library*.

The old man nodded. "That's a sizable collection of books. Have you ever discussed them with anyone?"

Henry said they weren't the kind of things you discussed.

"Why not?"

Because Sy said so.

The brushes over the doctor's eyes went up for a moment, then fell back into place. "Go on."

Sy said you had to keep the things you take seriously to yourself. Then Henry asked the doctor for some more money.

"I don't want to play that game right now, Henry. I'd like to hear whatever it is you feel like saying. If you don't want to say anything, that's fine too."

Henry said the word is one in silent grace.

"While it was yet the depth of His thought, the word which first emerged revealed a mind which speaks." The doctor finished the sentence for him. "You see. I know it too."

Henry asked for another quarter.

"Okay," the doctor said. He leaned over again and took out his change purse.

Henry asked the old doctor if he had foreknowledge of the Perfect Mind.

The old man was silent for a moment. Then he smiled and said, "Only as far as it dwells within us as an image of God."

Henry wanted to ask what that meant but before he could Dr. Alt asked Father Crowley if he'd ever met Henry's father.

"No. I missed both chances. It's too bad. I might have gotten to the bottom of things."

Dr. Alt turned back to Henry. "Would you like to tell me a little about what it's like to live in Atlantic City? It's a place I've never been to."

Henry didn't know what to say.

"Can you describe it to me?"

Henry said yes and he could get to the bottom and *underneath* too.

Dr. Alt chuckled and looked at Father Crowley. "Please do."

There were cisterns and basilicas all over Byzantium but there was only one that was called the Basilica Cistern because it was built underneath the Stoa Basilica, which was between the Phosphorion Harbor and the Forum of Constantine. It supplied water to the Palace and was so big and dark inside that you had to have a boat to get around and torches to light the way. It had three hundred thirty-six huge columns topped with Corinthian capitals and a high, vaulted ceiling, but instead of mosaics as decoration there was only moss and fungus and other things that grew in dark, wet places, and instead of the sound of prayers and the smell of incense all you could hear was a steady dripping and lapping of water and all you could smell was a cold, fertile dampness.

The priests didn't say anything. They waited for Henry to continue.

Once Henry's father took him through it. In a *boat*.

"Is that so?" the old doctor said and leaned forward a little.

Henry nodded.

"What were you doing there?"

Looking for corpses.

"Corpses? Why would you want to do that?"

Enemies of the Palace were dumping them into the water to ruin it for drinking. The boat had a long, curved prow and they built a fire in a large clay pot in the middle of the boat that gave off as much light as twenty torches. An old Armenian freed slave guided the boat through the underground caverns and told Henry to keep his eyes open because if you fell asleep underground you might never find the way back out.

"A fascinating story, young man. Is there more?"

Henry nodded and told them about a monk who came to Byzantium because his order was being persecuted and he and the other monks who lived with him in the wilderness agreed that the only way to stop the persecution was to petition the emperor. The emperor was away at his retreat on the Black Sea with his generals.

"What kind of monk?"

Henry said he didn't know but maybe a Montani or a Sabbatiani or one of those kinds that were always being persecuted. Procopius said the emperor had to keep tabs on the monks because they could make trouble. They got ideas because they had so much time to think and if they began to write them down and spread them around things could go bad fast. The streets of Byzantium were filled with monks and priests and ordinary people who were persecuted and forced to give up their beliefs but most people had either given up their beliefs because they didn't make sense anymore or they were like Sy and believed in everything because they were afraid to rule anything out.

"That's very interesting," Dr. Alt said.

Henry said it didn't matter if you were a Christian or a Jew. When you worked at the Palace you had a job to do and everyone was happy that way.

"What about Sy? I'd like to hear more," Dr. Alt said.

Henry said well, Sy was sort of like a monk, and he was a blackjack dealer too.

"Henry is a great storyteller, Father. But his stories are very confused," Father Crowley said.

Dr. Alt said, "That's all right. Go on, Henry."

Henry said Sy didn't want to rule anything out and that made him different from everybody else and also he had a head for numbers. That's why the emperor gave him a Christmas present.

"Yes?"

Henry said Sy wasn't like most people at the Palace. He wanted to rule everything in and worked toward his full orgastic capacity by sitting in a box so that he could feel the pulse of the universe.

Dr. Alt laughed. "That's marvelous. Did you hear that, Father?"

Father Crowley stood up and walked to the other side of the room. "I did, and I don't want to hear any more of that kind of talk, young man."

Dr. Alt waved his hand. "Don't worry, Father. He's just talking like a Reichian!" The old doctor laughed. "Did Sy talk about orgastic capacity?"

Henry nodded.

"Could you tell me more about what happened around the Palace?"

Henry said sometimes he made the rounds with his father. People respected a family man. Being a family man put everyone at ease. Henry said his father told him when people feared you and you made them feel comfortable anyway you could tell them to do anything and they'd do it.

"Now, *that's* a charming piece of psychology," Father Crowley said and sat down again. "What do you make of this kind of talk, Doctor?"

"Henry should feel comfortable to speak his mind."

Father Crowley rubbed his eyes and looked at his watch.

"What kinds of games did you play? You did play games, didn't you?"

Henry told him about plague sowing. The old man listened but this time he didn't laugh or say anything. "What other sorts of things did you do?"

Henry said he liked to go down to the Olympic swimming pool in the morning and watch Theodora swim because she looked like Porphyrius the whale.

"You mean Porphy the whale?"

Henry said no, Porphyrius. She was purple, like the great column in the Forum of Constantine.

"Has he told you this before?" Dr. Alt asked Father Crowley.

"I've heard some version of it," Father Crowley said. "I've heard so many different stories that nothing makes sense to me anymore. Tell us about Porphyrius, Henry. That's something I can't make heads or tails of. Henry talks about a whale named Porphyrius."

"That sounds very interesting. Could you tell me something about Porphyrius?"

Henry said whales are beautiful creatures.

"Have you ever seen one?"

Henry said yes.

"Where?"

Henry said in the Sea of Marmara.

"How interesting. When were you at the Sea of Marmara?"

Henry said he used to go there every morning to watch her swim.

"The fish is an extremely interesting and very powerful symbol," Dr. Alt said to Father Crowley. "I wrote about it in my book, *Psychosis as Excursus*."

"Oh?" Father Crowley said. He seemed only half interested.

"It's too complex to go into right now. But it is very significant."

"Do you think now is the right time to talk about it?" Father Crowley nodded at Henry.

"Of course! I want everything to be in the open. The fish is an archetypal symbol of the self, *de profundo lavatus*, drawn from the deep. As such it is an expression of psychological wholeness." He rubbed his palms together. "Very nice, Henry. This is a *very* good place to begin."

Henry said whales aren't fish.

"That's correct," Dr. Alt said, and smiled. "From the standpoint of zoology. But the psyche rarely takes taxonomic distinctions into account in elaborating its symbols."

"Dr. Alt is a very learned man, Henry. You might try listening to him. Stop talking like a smart aleck."

Henry looked into the fire for a few minutes. His angel called to him and his vision darkened and his head felt light. The angel's voice made a melody of the crackling logs and when the music faded and his vision returned, Henry looked at the old doctor and said nothing. Father Crowley stood up again and walked over to the fireplace and stood with his back to it.

Henry told the old doctor about the Olympic swimming pool and Theodora in her purple bathing suit and cap and how his father hated her.

"Your father hated her?"

Henry nodded.

"Why?"

Henry said because she was very powerful and he never knew where he stood with her.

The priests glanced at each other, then back at Henry. "Is that all?" Dr. Alt asked.

Henry shook his head. She was a smart-ass MBA bitch and was squeezing him to death too.

"That's enough of that," Father Crowley said.

Dr. Alt held up his hand. "Is Theodora the fish?"

Henry said not a fish, a whale. She swam every morning in the Olympic swimming pool and sometimes he saw her at the Golden Gate.

"The Golden Gate?"

Henry said it was the gate at one end of the city that was built by Theodosius and it was the gate through which all conquering emperors entered the city. On one side it said, *Theodosius adorns this place after the doom of the usurper,* and on the other side it said, *He who constructed the Golden Gate brings in the Golden Age.* Then Henry stopped talking and looked past the two priests into the flames. He watched the red and orange tongues flicker and lap and strained to hear the music he had heard a few minutes ago. He wanted to ask them about hell but decided to wait until some other time. The emperor's retreat on the Black Sea came into his thoughts and the owl that lived in the tree and he wondered if the emperor had given his father the job.

It was quiet for a long time.

"What do you make of it all?" Father Crowley asked.

The doctor took off his glasses and cleaned them. "Extremely interesting. But it is going to take time to sort things out." Then he put his glasses back. "Very well, then. I'd like to say a few things. This might not make much sense to either of you, but I just want to express what I think is happening here."

"Are you sure you want to do this?" Father Crowley asked.

"Absolutely. I want Henry to hear everything I have to say. Normally, you see, the relationship between the specific contents of the conscious and the unconscious becomes clear only in later stages of analytic treatment. But this situation is unique. I've never seen anything remotely like it. The overt confusion of conscious and unconscious facts seems to lead, well—straight to the later stage." He stopped for a moment. "It's hard to explain, and I know I'm talking past you right now, but it helps me to focus my thoughts. The situation is a difficult one. Extremely complex. Very interesting."

Henry looked into the fire.

"Of course, I'm speaking very generally and extemporaneously. What I say should not be taken as a diagnosis of any sort."

"Of course," Father Crowley said.

"But it is an extremely interesting situation, and I would like to get to know Henry better as a patient. Do you think that is possible?"

"I doubt there will be any objections," Father Crowley said. "Would you like to talk to Dr. Alt on a regular basis?"

Henry didn't want to talk to anyone but nodded just to get it over with.

Father Crowley looked at his watch and said, "Looks to me like it's time for lunch."

Henry asked to go to the bathroom.

"Run along. We'll be in the dining room. And don't forget to wash your hands." The two priests walked down the long corridor that led to the dining room and the other parts of the rectory. When they were out of sight Henry slipped out the front door and ran faster than he'd ever run before. A taxicab turned onto the street just as he reached the end of the block and Henry waved to it.

"What's the problem, kid?" the driver said.

Henry took out a hundred-dollar bill and showed it to the driver and asked him to take him to a store in Philadelphia called Mitzi.

The driver laughed.

Henry took out another hundred-dollar bill and showed it to the driver.

The driver stared at Henry and at the money. "Hop in," he said and opened the door.

EGYPT

Henry sat in the rear seat of the car and watched the back of the driver's head. They drove for a little while and Henry tried to open the window but it didn't work. The driver turned onto a highway and said something but Henry didn't hear because he was scared. The driver started to sing. "They often call me Speedo, but my real name is Mr. Earl." Then he looked into the rearview mirror. "C'mon up front," he said and patted the seat next to him.

Henry shook his head.

"Aw, c'mon. I can't see you sitting all the way back there."

Henry climbed over the seat.

"What's your name, boy?"

Henry told him.

"Pleased to meet you, Henry," Mr. Earl said. They drove for a long time. Mr. Earl smoked cigarettes and pointed to some factories and steel mills as they drove past. "The only thing worse than a mill in full production is an abandoned one," he said. "The world is unfair no matter how you look at it. It's getting worse too. Never thought I'd see it that way, but there it is. Time was, all I wanted was to stay alive." Mr. Earl rolled the window down and flicked another cigarette out onto the road. "But that was wartime, and I don't like to think about it, and I don't know if it even counts anymore. Probably not." A little while later he pulled into a rest area that had some picnic tables. "I'm starving," he said.

Mr. Earl was very tall and had big shoulders and a big chest and long reddish hair that he kept tied in a ponytail. He had a thick mustache that drooped down each side of his mouth, which he smoothed and twisted with his fingers a lot, and a jagged purple stain just under one of his eyes that looked like a tear that had never been wiped away. He wore big black boots and a jacket with lots of pockets. Henry thought Mr. Earl was only being friendly because he was going to kill him. Then he remembered what his angel had told him about the children of the heavenly man and how they too had passed through the degradation of the life of the flesh and suddenly Mr. Earl appeared to Henry as a man who had already passed through those degradations and they had made him harmless. Mr. Earl unpacked things from the trunk of the car and said he was preparing a feast.

Inside the trunk was an entire kitchen. There was a stove with two burners and a large wooden cutting board that folded up and out like a shelf. There was a jug with a faucet for water and there were drawers and containers built into the sides of the trunk. Mr. Earl said he did a lot of camping and whistled as he mixed things together and cut and chopped. In a little while he lifted up a large plate and closed the trunk. It was cold and the wind was blowing but Henry and Mr. Earl ate the whole omelette. Then they packed everything up again.

After eating Henry felt tired and he got into the back seat of the car. Mr. Earl said he had to take a leak and went to the restroom. Henry fell into a deep sleep. In his sleep he was herded through the crowded streets of Atlantic City with flocks of sheep and cows and children and slaves and captured soldiers. The closer he came to Caesar's Palace the denser the crowd around him became. Nothing was visible and in the darkness he was overwhelmed by the heat of so many bodies pressing against him. Then a bird came down from the sky and landed on Henry's shoulder. The crowd slowly disappeared and he found himself standing on the shore looking out to sea. The surf made no sound and there were no boats on the water. The hotels and casinos rose up behind him and there was perfect silence.

Henry woke up in the parking lot outside Egypt. He sat up and looked out the window. It was dark and there were only a few cars in the lot. Across the street was a building with a red neon sign that flickered on and off. There were no windows. A car drove by. It slowed down as it passed in front of Egypt but then it sped away and the street was silent again. Henry was frightened. The darkness around him was not sweet and it was cold inside the car. He began to cry.

Mr. Earl opened the door and got in. "What's the matter, Henry?" He took some things out of his pockets and put them in the glove compartment. "Listen, Henry. I need to ask you a favor. That money you paid me? You know, for the ride? Well, I owed somebody and now I'm broke again. Could you lend me a little more? I'm in a tight spot."

Henry felt in his pocket and took out a hundred-dollar bill and gave it to Mr. Earl and said that was all he had.

"Listen, forget it, kid," Mr. Earl said. "I don't want to take all you have."

Henry said it was okay.

"Tell you what," Mr. Earl said. "I'll take fifty."

Henry looked out the window at the sign flashing E-G-Y-P-T. EGYPT. E-G-Y-P-T. EGYPT. Mr. Earl waited for a moment, then said, "Why don't you come inside with me. I'll introduce you to Pearl."

Henry asked who Pearl was.

"An old friend," Mr. Earl said. "Come on in and find out for yourself." They walked across the dark parking lot and then Henry remembered that Egypt was where Mohammed Ali was from and that Helena had said he was going to take her there. Suddenly he was very glad and ran to catch up with Mr. Earl. When they entered, Henry's heart pounded and his ears rang. It was dark inside like a

HENRY OF ATLANTIC CITY

cave and very smoky—not like a place where books were hidden but like a place where they were forgotten.

"Meet my friend Henry," Mr. Earl said.

"Hello, Henry," Pearl said. She put an arm on his shoulder and drew him against her. "Cute little thing," she said to Mr. Earl. "Where'd he come from?" Her voice was raspy and she was pretty in a grown-up kind of way. She was wearing a halter top like the kind Helena wore at the health club in Philadelphia that made her bosoms plump out, and she had a small tattoo of a butterfly on the back of one shoulder.

Mr. Earl took out the money Henry had given him. "How about some change?"

Pearl went behind the bar and came back with two fifty-dollar bills and gave them to Mr. Earl. Mr. Earl put one in his pocket and gave the other one back to Henry and winked. "Thanks for the loan, pal."

Pearl gave Henry a Coke to drink. There was a TV set up above the bar that nobody was watching and a jukebox that played loud music. There was a pool table that nobody was playing at and there were booths with red lightbulbs in them where nobody was sitting. Egypt was nearly empty.

Mr. Earl put his arm around Pearl's waist and kissed her on the mouth.

Pearl pushed him away. "What breeze blew you in here?" she asked.

Mr. Earl shrugged his shoulders. "Just felt like seeing you." Mr. Earl drank some more and became serious. So did Pearl. They talked about someone they knew who had died. "I'm feeling older and lonelier than ever," she said. "All I need now is to get sick."

"That's enough of that," Mr. Earl said and went to the cigarette machine. While he was gone Pearl looked at Henry and smiled and kept looking at him but didn't say anything. Then when Mr. Earl came back she began to cry. Mr. Earl put an arm around her shoulder. "Jesus, kid. What did you say to her?"

Henry said nothing.

Pearl put her head on Mr. Earl's shoulder. "I'm glad you came," she said. Just then a door burst open and a woman came rushing into the room. She was barefoot and had on only underwear and her hair was all wild. Pearl stood up and the woman ran into her arms and began to cry.

"He tried to hurt me," the woman said.

Mr. Earl jumped up. "Who did? Where is he?"

"Shush. You stay out of this," Pearl said and patted the woman's head. But Mr. Earl ran out of the room. Then he came crashing back through the door holding a man in a headlock. The man was kicking and shouting and Mr. Earl kept saying, "Shut up!" and smashing his knee into the man's face. The man was bleeding and his arms were flailing. Mr. Earl dragged him to where the woman and Pearl were sitting. "This him?"

The woman nodded and ran back through the door and slammed it behind her.

"Just get him the hell out of here!" Pearl said.

The man groaned and Mr. Earl dragged him outside.

"Everything's just fine, everybody. Let's just forget it," Pearl shouted. Then she took Henry by the hand. "Come with me, sweetheart," she said. They went down a long corridor and up some stairs into an apartment. She turned on the TV set. "I'll be back up a little later," she said. "Make yourself at home."

Henry lay down on the sofa and tried to remember everything he knew but he couldn't remember anything. On the wall above the TV was a broken cuckoo clock. The door was open and the bird was showing but the hands of the clock didn't move. He wanted to get up and look around but he was scared and didn't want to get lost. His angel told him that damnation was a wordless, thoughtless frenzy of animal living.

When morning came Henry was still scared. He was lying in a big, soft bed in a room filled with wild animals, but then he saw that they were all stuffed. There were lots of birds that weren't singing and a fox that wasn't hunting and squirrels that weren't climbing and a deer that wasn't running and even butterflies that weren't flying because they were pinned to the wall. There were long blue drapes over the windows made to look like a waterfall and the wallpaper was a gigantic photograph of a deep forest in the summertime. He lay in bed as the waterfall became lighter and lighter until it was almost transparent. Then the silence of the forest became oppressive and when he clapped his hands to fill the void and the wide-eyed animals remained frozen in their places he remembered that he was in Egypt.

Henry put on his shoes and opened the door. He tip-toed down a short hallway and opened the door at the end.

"Who's that?" Mr. Earl said and sat up straight. Then he said, "Shit," and rubbed his eyes.

"What's going on?" Pearl was lying next to him.

"Never *ever* sneak up on me like that, kid."

Henry said he wanted to go to Philadelphia.

"Yeah, yeah, yeah. I know." He lay back down and pulled the covers up. "Go back to bed."

Pearl told Henry to wait in the hallway while she got dressed. Then she took him into the kitchen. "I'm going to cook you up a breakfast you'll never forget," she said. "How did you like sleeping in the Garden of Eden?"

Henry said the animals all looked dead.

"Well, we sure couldn't have *live* ones in there." Pearl lit a cigarette and smoked it while she made breakfast. "Say, how'd you like to come with me to my favorite place in the whole world? Can you guess where my favorite place is?"

Henry said he didn't know.

"The zoo! They have *live* animals there." Then she started to sing, "If we could talk to the animals, learn their languages da da da da de da de de de. Ah, shit. I always forget the words." She kept cooking and began to glow and shine and no longer looked cast into the mud like a tired woman who smelled smoky and sour like old men smell. The smell of food filled the kitchen and Mr. Earl came into the room.

"Smells good," he said. "And *wow*, do I have a headache!" He looked even bigger without his shirt on and he scratched himself and yawned and thanked Henry for waking him up like that. Then he grabbed Pearl and began to kiss her.

Pearl dropped her cigarette on the floor. "Let go," she said and bent down to pick it up. "I'm taking Henry to the zoo."

Henry asked Mr. Earl if he had killed the man last night.

Pearl gave Mr. Earl an angry look. "You just forget about what you saw last night, Henry. You're too young to understand."

"That's right," Mr. Earl said.

Pearl cracked some eggs into a bowl. "Now, go get cleaned up," she told Mr. Earl.

For breakfast they had pancakes and maple syrup and ham and Mr. Earl had three fried eggs on top of his pancakes.

When they were finished eating Henry said he didn't want to go to the zoo; he wanted to go to Philadelphia.

Pearl and Mr. Earl looked at each other. Then Mr. Earl said, "There's been a slight change of plan, kid. Pearl's taking you to Philadelphia."

"The Philadelphia Zoo," Pearl said.

Henry said he didn't want to go to the zoo; he wanted to go to Sy's sister's store.

"Don't worry about it, kid. Pearl wants to take you to the zoo first," Mr. Earl said.

Henry felt in his pocket and realized his money was gone. He ran into the Garden of Eden and tore the sheets off the bed and looked underneath it but didn't find anything. Then he went back into the kitchen and told Mr. Earl to give it back.

Mr. Earl was pouring whiskey into his coffee. "Give what back?"

Henry said his money.

"You accusing me of taking your money?"

Henry said yes.

"You can blame anyone you want, kid. But it ain't going to get you your money back." Mr. Earl sipped his coffee and smacked his lips together. Then he poured more whiskey into it. "Happens to me all the time. I've even got a system for dealing with it."

Henry asked what the system was.

"It's complicated," Mr. Earl said.

Henry said you stole my money!

"Are you calling me a thief?"

Henry said yes.

"Well," Mr. Earl said, "you'll have to prove it. Innocent until proven guilty. That's the law of the land, kid." Then he took a big gulp of coffee and went, AHHHH. "You shouldn't go pointing fingers at people unless you're sure about what you're saying."

Henry ran back into the Garden of Eden and closed the door and cried.

Pearl came to get him. "What's wrong?"

Henry told her Mr. Earl had stolen his money and wouldn't give it back. Pearl was all dressed up. She looked like a picture in a magazine, and tall because she was wearing boots and her hair was piled up underneath a big floppy hat. "Don't worry, Henry. I'll straighten it out." She took Henry into the kitchen. "Give Henry his money back," she told Mr. Earl. "I want to get going."

Mr. Earl sipped from his coffee cup. The jagged purple stain under his eye looked dark—almost black. "I don't have Henry's money."

Henry began to cry. Pearl took his hand. "Don't cry," she said and stroked Henry's hair softly like he imagined a mother would. He stopped crying. Then she stood up. "Now, let's get going!"

Outside the sunlight was blinding. Henry shielded his eyes in the crook of his arm.

"It's a perfect day," Pearl said. She opened the door to a pure white Cadillac Eldorado and told Henry to climb in. Inside everything smelled like perfume and the seats were red and soft.

Henry had to kneel on the seat and look out the back window because he couldn't see out the front window sitting down. Egypt looked different in the daytime. It looked like an old warehouse on a street filled with old warehouses and empty lots. Henry asked Pearl where they were.

"No-man's land," she said. They drove without talking and pretty soon signs began to appear on the road that said *Philadelphia* and Henry was glad. He knelt on the seat and looked out the back window and watched everything disappear behind them in straight lines.

The zoo was a crowd of names and cages and all Pearl did was pull Henry along by the hand and point. She bought a giant balloon on a string and a bag of peanuts and kept saying how much fun it was. She gave the balloon to Henry but he let it go.

"Why'd you do that?"

They stood and watched the balloon go up and up until it was a tiny speck in the sky. "Are you satisfied?" Pearl asked.

Henry said the image must rise again through the image.

She took him to see *Panthera leo* and *Panthera tigris* because Pearl said she loved cats. "Go ahead," she told him. "Stand up on the rail if you want. Help you see better."

Henry said he could see everything just fine.

"But all you're seeing is the sign!"

Henry said that was all he needed.

"But the animal is in the cage, dummy! That's just a sign." Then she pulled him away and they continued through the zoo. They went inside a big building where *Varanus komodoensis* lived with what remained of its whole suborder of *Suaria* of the class *Reptilia*. There were other suborders too. *Serpentes, Chelonia,* and a few of the genus *Crocodylus,* where Pearl stopped and looked for a long time. "I don't know what scares me more," she said. "Being eaten by a crocodile or squeezed to death by a snake. I guess being eaten by a crocodile scares me less because the idea of being swallowed whole is too terrible to even imagine. If I had my way there wouldn't be any snakes in the whole world."

Henry said there are many animals in the world in human form.

Pearl pulled some pins out of her hair and put them in again and adjusted her hat. Then she ate some peanuts and stared at Henry. Her eyes were fixed but her jaw moved and her silence hovered over him. Henry turned toward the glass case and read: *Crocodiles are not related to any other group of reptiles and derive from an evolutionary line of dinosaurs that did not become extinct. Crocodiles and their relatives resemble mammals in having a four-chambered heart. All other reptiles have a two-chambered one. This increased pulmonary efficiency gives the crocodile a great advantage as a predator.*

When he looked up Pearl was walking toward the door. She threw the bag of peanuts into a garbage can and brushed the bits of shell from the front of her coat. As she walked her whole body swayed and so did the floppy brim of her hat. Henry ran after her but when he caught up she turned and shook her finger at him. "If you keep following me, I'll go tell a guard. They know how to deal with runaways," she said.

Henry watched her as she walked through the door of the Reptile House and out into the sunlight. He began to cry. He tried to stop but couldn't. His stomach shook and he felt hungry even though he didn't want to eat anything. He stood there in the entrance to the Reptile House and the tears just kept coming. Then snot began to run from his nose and got smeared across his face. He forgot about the degradation of the flesh. He forgot about the angel in his ear. He forgot that he was a saint. Every passage of every gospel and book he'd ever read was useless to him. He even forgot about Father Crowley and Dr. Alt and the O'Briens—even though they were probably looking for him. He looked out into the sunlit zoo and had no idea where he was.

Then his angel spoke to him. It said everything bound together eventually comes unbound, whether it is a mother from her child or just cars passing each other on a busy highway.

What about Pearl? he asked the angel.

The angel said a pearl is the precious deposit that oysters form around a grain of sand and keep hidden inside themselves. It takes a long time to make, and the older and uglier the oyster the more beautiful the pearl inside.

Henry asked why.

The angel said because when you spend your whole life making something beautiful, it makes you ugly.

People were starting to look at him. One lady asked him if he was lost. He stopped crying and went back into the Reptile House and started reading the signs again so nobody would think he was lost. The first sign he stopped in front of said, *Sphenodon punctatum, also called the Tuatara, is the sole survivor of the order Rhynchocephalia, a group that has characteristics more primitive than those of lizards. Surviving unchanged for more than one hundred million years, Sphenodon punctatum exhibits one of the slowest rates of evolution known.*

Henry climbed up on the rail and looked into the glass case. *Sphenodon* was resting on top of a flat rock with one tiny eye fixed on him. Henry looked straight into the little eye and recognized the angel that lived there as the same one that lived in his ear. He tapped on the glass. The lizard didn't flinch. Suddenly the voice of a man said, "Get down from there."

Henry climbed down.

"Where are your parents, son?"

Henry said nothing.

"Are you lost?"

Henry said nothing and turned to look at *Sphenodon punctatum* again. The guard reached out to take Henry's arm but Henry ran. He darted through the crowd. The guard shouted, "Come back," and stayed close behind at first but Henry got away because the guard was too fat to keep up.

Henry ran in the direction of *Panthera leo* and *Panthera tigris*. "Stop! Come back here," the guard shouted. But Henry kept running as fast as he could. He ran into the Fish House. It was dark and quiet and the tanks glowed. He went into a room on one side of the hall. It was dark and he stopped to catch his breath. A small plaque on the wall glowed and was the only light in the room. The plaque said *Myctophidae: the family of deep-sea fishes having phosphorescent light organs.* Henry looked all around for the fish but the room was empty. There were no tanks and no other people. Only a plaque on the wall that glowed. Henry continued reading. *At eight hundred meters (two thousand six hundred feet) the effects of sunlight disappear. This is the depth where the luminous fishes live.*

Then a movie started and a voice said, "The room you are standing in approximates the light conditions at eight hundred meters. The atmospheric pressure at this depth is so great that scientists have only recently been able to send down equipment capable of withstanding the conditions." Then a tiny glow appeared on the screen. It was *Myctophidae*.

Henry remembered going down to the Sea of Marmara to watch for Theodora. He used to imagine what it would be like to be a whale and to live underwater and when he imagined that he always imagined a mother whale swimming ahead and guiding his way through the deepest depths of the ocean. Then he remembered that it is not possible for anyone to see anything of the things that actually exist unless he became like them—even *Myctophidae*, who were as fallen and lived as far from the light as any creature in this world and whose name meant snake nose because they were so ugly and forsaken their nose was a lantern which lighted their way.

Henry began to cry again. Then he began to feel sick. He sat down on the floor and watched the rest of the movie about *Myctophidae* and the other fishes of the darkness. There were fish with tubular eyes that were pointed upward to catch the light and fish with retinas made entirely of tiny golden rods that were sensitive only to the blue light of the spectrum because that was the last light to make it down so far. There was a fish called *Ipnops* that scientists thought had no eyes at all until they discovered a tiny plate on top of its head covered with retinal cells. There were fish with teeth like daggers, spears, and sabers and jaws big enough to eat anything they bumped into. The voice in the movie said scientists were trying to devise ways of bringing these specimens up to the surface so they could study them. The conditions the fish lived in were so severe that bringing them up would destroy them unless special methods could be devised. The voice said that even though scientists had learned a great deal it would be years before they knew all there was to know about these strange and bizarre creatures from the deepest depths of the ocean.

After the movie was over Henry stayed in the room and tried to adjust to the dark. But even with the plaque glowing he couldn't get used to it so he got up and left. The coast was clear and he left the Fish House. It was still a bright, sunny day outside and he was blinded. The daylight hurt. He rubbed and rubbed his eyes and waited until he could see again. Then he went to look for Pearl. He walked and walked but saw no sign of her. Then he went to where the car had been parked and found that it was gone.

There were lots of places in the zoo to hide, and it was easy to fool the guards by following along behind a family and pretending he was the straggler. Then the zoo closed and Henry found a room with buckets and mops and stayed in it for a long time. When it got dark he left the closet and snuck around. Most of the animals were asleep but there were plenty awake too. Henry read all the plaques. In the zoo things were scary only when they didn't have a name. As soon as they were named they weren't scary anymore. That was the power of names. Even *Myctophidae* was less scary once you knew its name. Henry tried to imagine what the scientist thought who saw *Myctophidae* for the first time. He imagined it was as scary as anything that had ever happened since the beginning of the world before anything was named.

When it was morning Henry found a telephone in the office near *Gorilla gorilla*. He used it to call Sy's sister at Mitzi.

"Oh my God! Henry, where are you? Are you all right?"

Henry said he was at the zoo.

"The zoo? What are you doing at the zoo?" Before Henry could answer she said, "Never mind. I'll be there in ten minutes. Meet me at the front entrance. Do you know where that is?"

Henry said yes.

"The whole world is looking for you, Henry. Everyone is worried sick."

Henry said promise you'll come?

"I'm leaving this minute. Be at the front gate."

Henry hung up the telephone and went to say good-bye to *Gorilla gorilla*. There was a whole family of them but one was in a cage all by herself. The man who fed her called her Big Nekkid. Henry felt sorry for her because she was all alone. He watched from a hiding place when the man went to feed her. "C'mon here, you Big Nekkid," he said and left food for her. While Big Nekkid was eating in one part of the cage the man closed it off and cleaned up the mess in the other part. The plaque on the cage said, *The relationship between gorillas and human beings, as measured biochemically, is so close that if they were members of any other group of organisms they would almost certainly be classified as members of the same genus despite their morphological differences.*

Big Nekkid was lonely. Henry could tell by the way she chewed, slowly and as if she didn't like the taste. After the man left Henry came out of his hiding place and opened up the door of the cage. Big Nekkid looked at

Henry and picked some things off her leg. She was so surprised that she went and sat down at the other end of the cage and put some branches in her mouth as if to say that she needed a minute to think. Henry said there are two trees in Paradise. The one bears animals, the other bears men. Adam ate from the tree that bore animals. He became an animal and he brought forth animals.

Henry waved good-bye to Big Nekkid and snuck through the zoo until he came to the front gate, where Sy's sister was already waiting in the car. Henry squeezed through the bars of the gate and when he got into the car Sy's sister grabbed him with both arms. "Thank God you're okay." Then she said Henry smelled awful and they drove off.

"How'd you get into the zoo?"

Henry said Pearl brought him.

"Who's Pearl?"

Henry said a pearl is the precious deposit that an oyster forms around a grain of sand.

Sy's sister took her eyes off the road and looked at Henry and shook her head. She told him about all the trouble he'd caused and how Father Crowley and the O'Briens and everybody including the state police were looking for him. "You've got a lot of explaining to do, kid." Then she pinched her nose with her fingers and said, "*Peeeyouuuu*, kid. You stink."

Big Henry was at Sy's sister's house when they got there. He came to the front door. "Hiya, Henry! How's it hangin'?" He was barefoot and wearing a bathrobe and holding a cup of coffee.

"Henry and I are married," Sy's sister said.

Big Henry put his arm around her and took a sip from his coffee cup and looked at Henry without saying anything.

"Go upstairs," Sy's sister said. "Get cleaned up before you stink up the whole house. You know where everything is."

"Good Christ, boy, you need to be disinfected," Big Henry said.

"And don't put the same clothes back on. I'll find something that will fit."

"Don't just stand there, boy. Go to it." Big Henry chased Henry up the stairs into the bathroom. He turned on the hot water full blast. After his bath Henry put on the new clothes Sy's sister gave him and looked at himself in the mirror. He remembered the words to the *Hymn of the Pearl*, which he had read in the Philadelphia Public Library. Suddenly the garment seemed to be a mirror of himself and Henry saw in it his whole self and his self apart and he understood that he was two entities yet one form.

That afternoon Helena and Mohammed Ali came over to see Henry. Helena's stomach was huge because she was going to have a baby and she looked older than Henry had ever imagined her to be. Prettier too. She ran up to Henry and hugged him and he bounced off her stomach like it was a hard rubber ball.

"Careful. Careful," Mohammed Ali said. He looked the same as before except now he was dressed in jeans and Henry had never seen Mohammed Ali in jeans before.

Henry asked Mohammed Ali where his Mercedes 450 SEL was.

Mohammed Ali laughed. "I don't have it anymore," he said. He took one of his gold-tipped cigarettes out of his shirt pocket and lit it. He blew a big cloud of smoke up at the ceiling.

Henry asked what kind of car he had now. Mohammed Ali took him outside to look.

"It's a Land Rover," he said. "A good family car. What do you think?"

Henry asked to get inside and Mohammed Ali let him get in and sit in the driver's seat. It was huge inside and Henry pretended he was driving across deserts and over mountains because Land Rovers were good cars for escaping in. Saints could be thrown into boiling oil or skinned alive. When that happened they became martyrs, but if they were lucky they escaped and found places to hide.

After a little while they went back inside. Henry was happy to see Mohammed Ali and Helena with a baby in her stomach. His angel was happy too and said no creation was so completely flawed that no good could come out of it.

"Are the O'Briens treating you badly?" Helena asked.

Henry said not only were they unable to detain the perfect man, they were unable to see him; for if they saw him they would detain him.

"Henry, this is serious. Everybody's in trouble."

Henry told Helena that her mother and Sy were married.

"I know," Helena said. "They're all in big trouble. Your father too. Did Mrs. O'Brien tell you?"

Henry said no.

"Do you know what a fugitive is?"

Henry said no.

"It's someone who is wanted by the police and who has to go underground."

Henry asked where underground.

"Nobody knows where. That's why they say underground. It means they have to live in hiding. If they're caught they'll be put in jail."

Henry said by coming into being the whole creation became enslaved forever, from the foundation of the world until now, and he fingered the chain his father had given him.

"Why did you run away?" Mohammed Ali asked.

Henry said because he wanted to live in Philadelphia.

Sy's sister came into the room. "The police are here."

Henry asked why she called the police.

"I didn't call them, Henry. They've been searching for you for two days."

The police took Henry into their car and made him sit in the back seat while one of them talked on the radio and the other one wrote in a book. It was a Ford Crown Victoria. Henry liked Mohammed Ali's Land Rover much better. In the Land Rover Henry could see out the window. The Ford Crown Victoria had bars on the window and all he could see was the backs of the policemen's heads. One policeman turned around. "What's your name, son?"

Henry said nothing.

"I asked you a question, son." The policeman had on a badge that said *Shumacher.*

Henry said nothing.

"Okay, son, let's get something straight. You've caused a lot of trouble. You can make it harder on yourself by not cooperating, or you can cooperate. Understand?"

Shumacher took Henry into a room at the police station and made him sit down until a woman came in and asked him some questions. She was wearing a badge that said *Farley.* "You feeling okay, Henry? You hungry?"

Henry shook his head.

"Anyone mistreatin' you? Hurt you in any way?"

Henry shook his head.

Farley took some papers out of a drawer and sat down on a bench in the office and asked Henry to sit down next to her. "I'm here to help you, Henry. It's my job to help children like you. But first you need to tell me why you ran away."

Henry said he didn't run away he fell away.

"You fell away?"

Henry said yes.

"Where did you fall from?"

Henry said from the light into the darkness.

Farley wrote down what Henry said on a pad of paper. "How did you fall? Did someone push you?"

Henry said no but in the creation when the darkness had mixed with the light and had darkened the light, the world became neither dark nor light but only weak.

Farley said, "Amen to that," and wrote on her pad. "Was you ever locked in your room?"

Henry said no.

"Does the dark frighten you?"

Henry said no one can see in the dark.

"Does that frighten you?"

Henry said not seeing is not knowing.

"Amen to that too. Where'd you hear that, Henry? You hear that in church?"

Henry shook his head.

"How 'bout in school? You hear that in school?"

Henry shook his head. Then he said if you are born a human being it is the human being who will love you. If you become a spirit it is the spirit which will be joined to you. If you become thought it is thought which will mingle with you. But if you become a horse or ass or bull or dog neither those who belong above nor those who belong within will be able to rest in you and you will have no part in them.

"Lord *a'mighty*," Farley said and looked at Henry for a few minutes. Then she wrote down a few things on her pad. "Now, tell me. You sure no one ever spanked you?"

Henry said no.

"Think real hard, Henry. Try to remember as far back as you can. Anyone ever hit you?"

Henry shook his head.

Farley wrote down some more. "Where you been hearin' all this talk, Henry? Church?"

Henry said from reading.

"You read a lot, huh?"

Henry said only when he had books to read. The rest of the time he remembered.

"I guess you remember a lot, huh?"

Henry said everything from the beginning.

Farley put her pen down and smiled. She was chubby and the uniform she was wearing made her look chubbier because it was ironed and stiff. She had a wide face and smooth dark skin and smelled a little like cough medicine. When she breathed the whole upper part of her body lifted up toward her chin. "I have children around your age, Henry. Come home filled with all *sorts* of ideas—things they maybe heard in school, saw on TV, read in books." She took both of his hands and held them in hers. She had a ring on her finger that looked too tight. It had a little diamond in it that twinkled under the fluorescent lights. She looked at Henry without saying anything, just looked at him and held his hands tightly. Henry saw that

Farley loved her children more than anything else in the whole world and that somehow made him feel sad. Then Shumacher came in and asked her to step outside with him for a minute.

When they came back into the room, Shumacher sat down behind the desk and took some things out of the drawer.

"I have to go," Farley said. "I'll be back in a little while. Don't worry. Everything's going to be all right."

When she left the room Shumacher looked up. "How'd you get to the zoo, Henry?"

Henry said he took a cab.

Shumacher nodded and looked at Henry for a few minutes without saying anything. "I've heard that you're a real wise guy," he said. "You can forget that crap with me. Okay? Now, how did you get to the zoo?"

Henry said he took a taxi.

"Where'd you get the money?"

Henry said he took it out of the kitchen drawer at the O'Briens'.

"How much did you take?"

Henry said he didn't know.

Shumacher asked a lot of other questions but Henry said he didn't know or he couldn't remember. Then Schumacher put down his pen and looked across the desk. "You seem pretty sure of yourself for someone who's in trouble. But maybe you don't realize just how much trouble you're in."

Henry looked at his shoe, which was untied. He was about to tie it when Shumacher slammed his hand down on the desk. "Look at me!"

Henry sat straight up. He was scared.

"Most kids who did what you just did are lucky to ever get back home. You know where most of them end up?"

Henry shook his head.

"With their pictures on shopping bags and milk cartons. Is that what you want? To see yourself on a milk carton or a shopping bag?"

Henry said nothing.

Then Shumacher shoved a drawer closed and pushed himself away from the desk. "You're not just a runaway, son. You're also a juvenile felon. Do you know what a felon is?"

Henry said nothing and just looked at Shumacher, who was staring at Henry with eyes like glass.

"A felon is someone who commits a crime punishable by law."

Henry said nothing.

"You think I'm just trying to scare you and send you home, don't you?"

Henry said nothing.

"I've got some bad news for you, kid. You want to take a guess what the bad news is?"

Henry said nothing but his heart began to pound and his face grew hot and he heard a ringing in his ears and fear spread inside him like a wordless blackness.

"Go ahead, Henry," Shumacher said. "Take a guess."

Henry shook his head.

"You remember that gorilla you let out of the cage at the zoo?"

Henry said nothing.

"Well, son, that gorilla is now dead thanks to you." Shumacher stood up behind his desk and looked straight at Henry. "Let that sink in a little," he said and took some papers from the desk and left the room.

Henry got up and walked around Shumacher's office like he was doing the stations of the cross. He thought about the time Sy took him and Helena out for a drive. They drove all over Atlantic City and Sy showed them the sights like it was a tour. They drove by the Hagia Sophia and the Hippodrome and the Absecon Lighthouse and the Forum of Constantine and the Convention Center and all the other important sights. They went to the drive-through at Burger King and drove around some more.

"Are you happy living alone?" Helena asked Sy.

"I'm happy just to know that such a thing as happiness exists *at all* in the emptiness of the universe," Sy said. "But it's all a question of scale, and once you begin *measuring*, how happy can you really be?"

When they got back to the Palace Sy pulled into the special place for limos at the main entrance. It was getting dark and a strong wind was blowing. You could hear the surf pounding in the distance, and being under the bright lights of the Palace's main entrance was like being on a great rostrum at the end of the world. Sy jumped up onto the hood of the car and shouted, "CAST INTO THE INFINITE IMMENSITY OF SPACES OF WHICH I AM IGNORANT AND WHICH KNOW ME NOT, I AM FRIGHTENED!" He was wearing his blackjack tuxedo and he adorned the big black car like a living ornament. The wind blew his hair back and his clothes tight against his body. "Ever heard of Pascal?" he asked as he jumped off the car.

Henry said there was a lady named Pascal who worked at the reception desk.

"Is there such a thing as *sort-of-happy*, or *happy-in-spite-of*?" Sy asked.

"Sure there is," Helena said.

"I don't think so," Sy said.

That was how Henry learned that most things in the world, as long as their inner parts are hidden, stand upright and live.

Shumacher came back into the room. "Well, son? Have things sunk in a little?"

Henry said nothing.

Shumacher sat at the desk and said if they hadn't maybe he could help Henry along a little. Then he opened up a folder and began to read: "5:30 A.M.: Gorilla keeper begins rounds of primate house according to schedule. 6:15: Keeper finishes morning feeding, returns to office. Notices office door left open. Nothing else unusual. 6:30:

Keeper leaves office to go to washroom, discovers gorilla cage door open. Returns to office immediately and calls zoo security to report escaped primate. 6:40: Accident reported on 34th Street. Driver reports seeing large animal crossing road, swerves vehicle to avoid collision, strikes car parked at curb. 6:53: Zoo authority reports escaped primate to city police. Police assist search effort. 7:30: Second accident reported on 34th Street. Police arriving on scene report injured gorilla. Driver reports animal ran in front of vehicle. Zoo officials informed. 7:40: Zoo officials arrive on scene. Gorilla unconscious, bleeding from head and upper torso regions. Zoo veterinarians remove animal from scene of accident. Vehicle sustained heavy damage to front fender and grill. Driver unhurt. 8:30: Zoo officials report animal dead of injuries."

Henry watched Shumacher close the folder and push it to the side of the desk. Henry's heart swelled inside his chest and he felt sorry but he didn't cry.

"Do you still think you're a funny guy?"

Henry said nothing.

"C'mon, son. Aren't you even sorry?"

Henry looked at the seventeen stations of the cross and said some neither desire to sin nor are able to sin.

"Oh. I suppose it was all just an accident? You just accidentally snuck into the zoo and accidentally let a gorilla loose?"

Henry said nothing.

"Get up," Shumacher said. He took Henry by the arm and they went down some corridors and through some doors. "I want you to see what happens to wise guys," he said. Then he took Henry on a tour of the prison. "Take a good look around, son. This is where all troublemakers eventually end up." They went down a corridor that was filled with cells and Shumacher winked at some policemen as they went past. They went to the end of the corridor and then turned around and walked all the way back. There were prisoners in all the cells. It was noisy and smelled bad. Shumacher stood with his hands on his hips staring at Henry. "Had enough?" he asked.

Henry said nothing.

"Let's go," Shumacher said. They went back to his office.

Father Crowley came a little while later. He had to sign some papers so Henry could leave the police station. "You should be ashamed of yourself," the priest said when they were in the car. "In my opinion, you deserve a good beating."

Henry asked where they were going.

"To straighten out the mess you've made," Father Crowley said.

Henry said for you descended into a great ignorance but you have not been defiled by anything in it. For you descended into a great mindlessness and your recollection remained. You walked in mud and your garments were not soiled and you have not been buried in their filth and you have not been caught.

The priest was silent for a few seconds and looked straight ahead and drove. "Where did you learn that?" he asked.

Henry didn't answer.

"I asked you a question, young man."

Henry said it was from a gospel.

"Which gospel?"

Henry said it was from the First Apocalypse of James.

The priest looked at Henry for a long time. "Do you realize that by speaking words you don't understand—by repeating blasphemies—you are sinning? Doing the work of the devil?"

Henry watched the tall buildings and the parks and the streets of Philadelphia through the side window. They stopped at a red light. "Nobody is free of sin, Henry. Sin is in the world everywhere, even if you aren't conscious of it. We all live in sin. It is the consequence of the Fall." They drove a little while longer and then Father Crowley said, "I wish you would read the true gospels. You might not be such a confused little boy." He was quiet again for a while. "Why do you insist on making it so hard for the people who are trying to help you? The O'Briens have given you a home and you show your thanks by running away? How do you expect to get along in life if you turn away from people? There are people who care all around you. You need to open your eyes." Then he stopped talking and just drove.

They went to Sy's sister's house. Father Crowley said he was glad to finally meet her. "Have you had any contact with the father?" he asked.

"None whatsoever," Sy's sister said. Then she looked at Henry with sad eyes. "What's going to happen to him, Father?"

"Frankly, I don't know. It's an extremely complicated situation—legally speaking. Never mind the rest."

"I've talked about it with my husband," Sy's sister said. "We'd like him to stay with us."

"That's very kind of you. But I'm afraid it won't be possible."

"Do you have a better place in mind?" Big Henry asked.

"He'd be well taken care of," Sy's sister said.

"That's very kind, and I don't doubt it for a minute," Father Crowley said. "But there are laws, and Henry's case is extremely complicated. The state has first to try to locate a parent. Then a court has to order parental rights to be terminated—which is another way of saying he's been abandoned. Right now Saint Jude's is the only place Henry can go."

"Saint Jude's?"

"It's a Catholic orphanage I'm involved with."

"An orphanage?" Sy's sister had tears in her eyes.

"On top of all that, there's the problem of what happened at the zoo." They talked for a long time but Henry stopped listening. He asked if he could go upstairs.

"Of course you can," Sy's sister said. "Lie down and take a nap."

"That's a very good idea," Father Crowley said. "I'll wake you up when it's time to leave."

Henry went to the room he had spent the summer in. Even with the door closed he could hear the grown-up voices droning downstairs. He lay down on the bed and watched the light make patterns on the ceiling. His angel was quiet because it was late afternoon and that was the time of day for quiet. In Byzantium in the late afternoon everything grew quiet too. Shopkeepers closed their stalls, porters put down their loads, artisans put down their tools, and the ships in the harbor lost their crews. Even the Palace became quiet. People dropped fewer coins into the slot machines; the roulette wheels spun less frequently. These were the hours when most guests arrived and checked into their rooms. They arrived in cars and on buses and even by limousine. If it was summer people came in off the beach.

He thought of his father and Sy and Helena's mother. If they were fugitives they were also suffering in a kind of way. Saints were fugitives too. They suffered because no matter where they were they could never forget the truth of their existence—even if they had to live their whole lives underground. It was like Sy said one day when he came to take Henry out for a walk along the beach. He said, "To be alive is to be subjected to the cruelty of facts." Living underground was a cruel fact.

He went to the window. It was sunny and cold outside. Father Crowley's black Chevrolet Malibu was parked at the curb in front of the house. A group of kids walked past it. One of them was carrying a stick and whacked the car on the hood. The kids didn't run away. They just walked down the street whacking parked cars along the way.

IV

SAINT JUDE'S

"It's a sad day for gorillas in Philadelphia," a voice on the radio said.

Father Crowley turned up the volume. "You listening?" he asked.

Henry looked out the window of the priest's Chevrolet Malibu and said nothing. The reporter said the gorilla's name was Omo and that Omo had been born in the zoo and had lived there for almost twenty years. He talked about how Omo had been loose for a few hours before getting hit and how the accident had backed up traffic during the morning rush hour.

"Do we have any more information on how the animal got loose?"

"Well, Sally, according to zoo officials, the cage was opened early this morning—apparently by a young boy who had somehow gotten into the zoo."

"A child?"

"That's right."

"Do you have a name?"

"No, Sally. Not yet."

"Does anyone know how the boy got into the zoo?"

"I don't have all the facts, Sally, but the police officer I talked to said it looks like a case of child abandonment."

"You mean the boy was abandoned in the zoo?"

"That's what I've been told. But again, zoo officials aren't commenting."

"Well, thanks, Scott. This certainly is a sad day for gorillas. Action News will keep you posted."

Father Crowley turned off the radio and didn't say anything.

After a while Henry asked Father Crowley about his stuff at the O'Briens' house.

"What stuff?"

Henry said his books.

"There are rules at Saint Jude's, Henry. We'll have to check first to see what you can bring with you."

Henry asked what Saint Jude's was.

"It's a home for boys," Father Crowley said just as they drove through a big gate with a cross on top. There was also a sign that said *Private Property* and one that said *No Trespassing*.

Saint Jude's was like being way out in the desert or high up in the mountains. Monasteries were always out in the wilderness. Procopius said the biggest troublemakers in Byzantium were sent to monasteries and almost none of them ever came back. Next to strangulation it was the best way of getting rid of enemies.

The head of Saint Jude's was a bald priest named Father Rogan. They went into his office and Father Crowley told Father Rogan all about what Henry did. Father Rogan didn't say much. He held his palms together with his fingertips under his chin and nodded his bald head and said, "I see." When they were finished talking, Father Rogan asked Henry if there was anything he'd like to know about Saint Jude's.

Henry asked the priest who Saint Jude was.

Father Rogan got up from his desk and walked over to the window and stood with his back to it. The window went all the way to the floor and the drapes were pulled aside so Henry could see out across the wide lawn. The front gate was just over a small hill and Henry could see the tip of the cross on top of it even though Father Rogan took up most of the window. He was wearing a cassock. "I've been here nearly twenty years and in all that time nobody has ever asked that question." He crossed his arms over his chest and went up on tiptoe and down again. "Saint Jude was one of the twelve apostles, Henry. He was the brother of the Apostle James of Jerusalem. Some scholars believe that James was Jesus' half-brother, which means that Jude could also have been a half-brother of Jesus. That, however, is not church doctrine. Jude was also called Lebbeus; Thaddeus; and Judas, the son of James.

Most commonly, he is called Judas *Not* Iscariot, to avoid confusing him with the Judas who betrayed Jesus to the Romans."

Father Crowley interrupted: "You should mention that we don't know whether Jude was the half-brother of James, as is written in the Epistle of Jude, or Judas the son of James."

"That is quite right," Father Rogan said. "Jude wrote an epistle. Do you know what an epistle is? An epistle is a letter. And in his letter, Saint Jude warned of the danger in accepting and being deceived by false teachings."

Father Crowley smiled and nodded. "Did you hear that, Henry?"

Father Rogan went to the bookshelf and took down a volume and opened it and read out loud from the Epistle of Jude: *"What defilement there is in their banquets, as they fare sumptuously at your side, shepherds that feed themselves without scruple! They are clouds with no water in them; driven before the winds, autumn trees that bear no fruit, given over anew unto death, plucked up by the roots."* He closed the book and stood there for a minute. Then he put the book back on the shelf. "Saint Jude was describing the emptiness of heretical teachings— including the idea that God is separated from creation." He went back to the window and put his hands behind his back. His dark eyes and his bald head made him look fierce. Henry had to look away.

Father Crowley took a deep breath and clasped his hands behind his head. Henry felt himself shrinking under the stares of the two priests. He said he who understands, let him understand.

Father Rogan wrinkled his forehead, then he looked down at the floor. "Where do you have that from?"

Henry said from the Gospel of Mary.

"There *is* no Gospel of Mary," Father Rogan said. "There are *four* canonical gospels: Matthew, Mark, Luke, and John." He took another book from the shelf and showed it to Henry. It was called *Confessions* by Saint Augustine. "This is one of the books we teach in high school. You'll read it when you're old enough to understand." He let Henry hold the book for a minute, then he took it away and put it back on the shelf. "Augustine was a great saint, but before he came to the one true God, he was a pagan and a Manichaean."

"Pay attention, Henry," Father Crowley said. "You have a lot to learn." He stood up and put a hand on Henry's shoulder. "I'll begin to make the arrangements," he said to Father Rogan and squeezed Henry's shoulder.

A man came in and Father Rogan introduced him as Mr. Miller. He took Henry by the hand. Father Rogan walked to the door with them and before they left he put his hand on Henry's head. "I want you to feel at home here, Henry." His smile made him look like a different person from the one who had stood like a shadow at the window a few minutes earlier. Henry wondered if that was how priests were different from saints. Priests were shadows, and saints were the surfaces that shadows were cast upon. "You're going to meet other boys and make friends. Pretty soon you'll feel like you're part of a big family. That's what we are here, Henry. A family. Isn't that right, Mr. Miller?"

Mr. Miller nodded. "That's right."

"There's one other thing you should know about Saint Jude," Father Rogan said before they left. "Saint Jude is the patron saint of hopeless causes."

Father Crowley cut in. "Because he shared the name of Jesus' betrayer, Judas Iscariot; and because of that devotion to him was neglected."

Father Rogan messed up Henry's hair. "That's exactly right, Henry. No need to worry. This is a community, and we all draw strength from each other. We share everything. Our joys and our sorrows. That's what makes us *strong*."

Mr. Miller squeezed Henry's hand. "C'mon, I'll show you around."

There were no saints at Saint Jude's, only dead bluesmen and rock-and-rollers. Elvis Presley, Jim Morrison and John Lennon and Keith Moon and Kurt Cobain and Pigpen and Sid Vicious, Robert Johnson and Howlin' Wolf and Honey Boy Edwards and Elmore James and Ernest Whiskey Red Brown and Otis Redding and Jimi Hendrix all lived at Saint Jude's. Henry knew their other names too but you weren't allowed to use them except in class. It was called an "err" if you did, and whenever you made an err the one you erred got to stomp on your foot as hard as he wanted to.

The first day after classes Elvis Presley and Otis Redding came up to Henry. "What's *your* name, dude?"

Henry told them.

"You have to have another name," Elvis said. He was the tallest of all the boys and had his own pair of scissors that he used to cut his hair.

"No talkin' to nobody 'til you get a name," Otis Redding said. He was a black kid with bad eyes and had to wear glasses. They had big square frames. He talked faster than anyone Henry had ever heard. "Not 'less someone talks to *you* first."

"If you don't have a name by the end of the week, *we'll* give you one," Elvis said.

"You don't want that," Otis Redding said.

"No way," Elvis said. They both laughed and went to the gym.

During free time you could go anywhere you wanted as long as you didn't leave the property. There was a big lawn that spread out from the main mansion and a small patch of woods behind the dormitory. Mr. Miller told Henry that Saint Jude's used to belong to a rich industrialist who had lived in the mansion all alone. When he died he left his house and all the property around it to the church and said it had to be made into a home for boys because he'd been an orphan. Mr. Miller said there were all kinds of rules that he had set up and that was why Saint

Jude's was so special. Except for the one dorm and the chapel they weren't allowed to change the place in any way. He said everyone had to get straight A's at Saint Jude's. If you didn't get straight A's you had to go somewhere else. There were no exceptions. Mr. Miller told Henry that he'd been a Saint Jude's boy and had always considered it his home. That's why he came back. He said the boys of Saint Jude's were special and Henry was lucky to be there.

Henry did everything he was supposed to and he kept his mouth shut. He went to classes and to the dining hall and to the gym. Instead of playing sports during free time he went to the library because it was quiet. He found the book Father Rogan had showed him and some other books by Saint Augustine. One was called *City of God* and there were some smaller books too. One was called *Against the Manichaeans* and the other was called *Of the Morals of the Catholic Church*.

At Saint Jude's Henry spent days as a blank. But not because his angel wouldn't talk to him. The angel in his ear talked more than ever and said things Henry didn't understand, like things are not imperishable but sons are and nothing will be able to receive imperishability if it first does not become a son. Sometimes as Henry lay under the covers or walked across the lawn toward classes or struggled to eat the food they fed him he would see himself being raised up into the sky on a cloud and the world would disappear beneath him. He would look down and see all the land and all the oceans. He would see everything in the world from the smallest to the biggest and nothing would be ugly or scary or strange but it would all be just so.

The boys didn't talk to him. He didn't have a name so everybody pretended he wasn't there.

At the end of the week Elvis Presley and Otis Redding came up to him and said he had to give his name tonight before lights out.

"I can see you tryin' *real* hard to be cool, muhfucker," Otis Redding said.

Henry looked past them at Mr. Miller, who was coming across the lawn toward them.

"Tonight, dude," Elvis said.

Mr. Miller jogged across the lawn. "There's someone here to see you, Henry. In Father Rogan's office."

"Well, well, well, young man," Dr. Alt said. He motioned for Henry to come toward him. "I hope you didn't think I was going to let you get away so easily."

Father Rogan was sitting at his desk looking at some papers and wearing reading glasses. "How are things going, Henry?"

Henry said they were fine.

"Good, very good," Father Rogan said. He took off his reading glasses. "Do you remember who Saint Jude was?"

Henry said Lebbeus whose surname was Thaddeus; Judas *Not* Iscariot; Judas, brother of James or Judas, son of

James of Jerusalem; Judas, half-brother of Jesus or nephew of Jesus; Jude, patron saint of hopeless causes.

Father Rogan put his papers down and pressed his glasses to his lips like he was kissing them. "That's very good, Henry. I understand why everybody is so interested in you."

Dr. Alt smiled and rolled his cane between his palms.

"Is there anything else you want to tell me before Dr. Alt gets started? We haven't seen each other since the day you arrived."

Henry shook his head.

"Are you sure? You've been here over a week now. There must be *something* you want to tell me about."

Henry said all I want to tell you is that I do not know where I came from when I was born into this life which leads to death—or should I say, this death which leads to life?

Father Rogan looked up over the rims of his glasses. "That's very interesting, Henry. Where do you have it from?"

Henry said Saint Augustine.

"Reading on your own, I see," the priest said. "Very good. But inappropriate. This isn't a time for pranks, young man." Then he took Dr. Alt and Henry down to the teacher's lounge, where they could talk in private.

"How do you like Saint Jude's?" Dr. Alt asked when they were alone.

Henry said it was okay.

Dr. Alt sat down in a black armchair that had a table next to it with a pile of books and magazines on it. He dropped his cane to the floor beside the chair and took off his glasses and cleaned them. "Would you like to tell me why you ran away?"

Henry looked at the old man and saw that he had some gold teeth in the back of his mouth.

"Running away never solves any problems. But it does require a certain amount of confidence." The priest finished cleaning his glasses and put them on again. "I'd like to hear about your adventure. Can you tell me how you got to the zoo?"

Henry told the doctor about going to the zoo and letting Big Nekkid out of the cage but he didn't tell about meeting Mr. Earl or Pearl or what happened in Egypt.

"Why did you let the gorilla out of the cage?"

Henry said he didn't know.

"I'm sure you don't," the old priest said. Then he smiled and showed his gold teeth. "Do you still remember *The Apocryphon of John* and the other things you told me about?"

Henry said he remembered everything.

"Do you remember your dreams?"

Henry said yes.

"Tell me about them."

Henry asked which dreams, the sleeping ones or the awake ones.

"Any ones you can remember."

Henry told Dr. Alt that he dreamed he was with his father and Sy and the Whore of Jersey City and Helena and they all lived on a boat together and sometimes Sy's sister and Big Henry came to visit.

"Is that an asleep or an awake dream?"

Henry said it was an awake one.

"Do you miss your father?"

Henry said I am not like him but I clothed myself with everything of his.

Dr. Alt took out a handkerchief and blew his nose. Then he folded it and put it back in his pocket. "Where did you hear that?"

Henry said the angel in his ear.

"Has the angel always been there?" Dr. Alt asked.

Henry said yes and without the angel in his ear he wouldn't know what to say or think. Every saint has to have an angel with wings to carry him away.

"Away from what?"

Henry said from all earthly things.

"I see." Dr. Alt smiled and his gold teeth showed again. "Sort of like a divine spark, right?"

Henry said in Greek the word *philosophy* means *love of wisdom.*

Dr. Alt laughed. "Yes. That's exactly right. What interests me is where the spark—or the wisdom—comes from. That's the most fascinating question I can think of. It's a beautiful mystery. It is what gives shape to my faith. I don't only think like a priest, you know. As a psychologist, I consider the words and pictures which occur in the mind to be an *epiphenomenon* of that mysterious spark."

Henry asked what an epiphenomenon was.

"I'm glad you asked. It's a Greek word too. It means something that arises out of but does not depend upon. Just as consciousness can be seen as a by-product of brain activity, words and symbols can be seen as an *epiphenomenon* of consciousness. You don't seek the meaning of a symbol in the *brain*. The brain just is. You look to consciousness and to the symbol itself." He stopped and smiled. "But I don't want to confuse you." He reached down and picked up his cane.

Henry asked Dr. Alt who his favorite saint was.

"Thomas Aquinas," the old priest said. "Maybe one day you'll learn about him."

Henry said his favorite was Saint Augustine. He asked if Thomas Aquinas had foreknowledge of the Perfect Mind.

Dr. Alt laughed. "I'm sure *he* didn't think so," he said. "Aquinas was a realist. He would not have claimed anything like that."

After the meeting Henry went back to the dormitory and lay down on his bed. He wondered what Dr. Alt would say if he told him about Mr. Earl and Pearl and figured it would only get him in trouble. He was glad he had kept his mouth shut but he hoped Mr. Earl and Pearl went to jail and were put to slow and painful deaths because they deserved it. It was like Sy said, you had to keep the

stuff you took seriously to yourself. Dr. Alt would probably agree with that.

Mr. Miller came in. "What are you doing here, Henry?
It's time for gym."

Henry stared at the ceiling and even though his eyes
were open he pretended he was sleeping.

"C'mon, Henry. Get up."

Henry kept looking at the ceiling. The angel in his ear
said the flesh will not rise.

"Are you feeling sick?"

Henry tried and tried not to repeat the angel's words
but he couldn't help himself so he said the flesh will not
rise.

"Very funny," Mr. Miller said. "If you're sick, you
should report it. You can't just go off by yourself without
saying anything to anybody." He put his hand on Henry's
forehead. "You don't have a fever."

Henry tried not to blink. His eyes began to water and
spots of blackness began to appear on the ceiling.

"I'll excuse you from gym today," Mr. Miller said. "Stay
here and take a nap. But you're not to leave the dorm. I'll
get you at dinnertime."

The angel said it is necessary to rise in the flesh since
everything exists in it.

Henry turned on his side. The beds were lined up one
next to the other with a small table beside each and a trunk
at the foot until the last one disappeared into the wall at the
end of the room. That was Otis Redding's bed. Henry could

hear the hum and echo of the empty dormitory and all he could see were the shadows that the late-afternoon light made coming in through the windows. He thought about his mother and wondered why his father had never told him her name or even that she was dead until that day when they were ice skating in New York City. Saint Augustine's mother was named Monica. He loved her very much and she cried and cried when he left Carthage and went to Rome. Truth is the mother, knowledge the father. Only he who has knowledge of the truth is free. Henry fell asleep and dreamed that he saw his mother. She was beautiful, with eyes set straight ahead into the future and all the secrets of her nature broken up into many little bits of colored stone.

That night Elvis Presley stood at the foot of Henry's bed and shouted, "Okay! Listen up!" When things got quiet he said, "It's name time, dudes!" He made Henry stand up on his bed. "What's your name?"

Henry didn't say anything.

"Tell us your name, dude," Elvis said.

Everybody laughed and someone said, "Yeah, faggot."

Ernest Whiskey Red Brown jumped up and down. "Faggot. Faggot. Faggot." Then John Lennon slammed his pillow into Ernest Whiskey Red Brown's face. They began to wrestle. Someone began to chant, "Fight, fight," and the two boys began to wrestle more seriously until Otis Redding told them to break it up.

"What the fuck do you think you're doing?" Otis yelled. He pushed them both backward onto their beds. "You want to get free time cut back again? Any of *my* free time gets cut because of you I'll kick both your asses!" He looked at Henry. "Same goes for you."

Henry lay down on his bed and looked up at the ceiling. Elvis grabbed him and tried to make him stand up again.

"That's enough," Otis Redding yelled. "Cut it out!" His voice was louder and deeper than any of the other boys', and since he was the oldest, Elvis Presley backed off. "Okay, dude, relax," he said and went back to his bed and threw himself down on it.

Otis Redding went down to the end of the room where his bed was. "We already lost fifteen minutes of free time because of *fuckin'* John Lennon over here," he said. "No way I'm gonna let it go to thirty. Not for any of you dumb *fucks*." Just as he lay down Mr. Miller came in. "Five minutes to lights out," he said.

The next day everyone was mad at everyone else and nobody paid any attention to Henry until night, when Elvis Presley came over to Henry's bed again. "Okay, dude, time's up. What's your name?"

Robert Johnson jumped up and down on his bed and sang, "I went down to the crossroad fell down on my knees." Then he fell back onto the bed and pedaled the air with his legs like he was riding a bicycle and strummed an invisible guitar across his belly.

163

"You finished?" Elvis asked.

Robert Johnson kept strumming the invisible guitar on his belly and singing, "I believe to my soul now, po' Henry sinkin' down."

"Well?" Elvis Presley demanded.

Henry said nothing.

"You have to have a name," Elvis said. He put his hands on his hips and tried to look tough. Then the other boys all came over and surrounded Henry's bed.

"C'mon. You can become anyone you want to. Anyone you ever wanted to be. It's easy."

"Where's Elmore?" Otis Redding said.

"Over here," Elmore James said.

"Why you sitting over there all by yourself? We got to get the new kid his name."

"Chill, man. Stop acting up," Elmore James said.

"What you thinking about, Elmore?" Otis asked.

"Gettin' the fuck outa here," Elmore James said.

"You always thinking too hard. That's a problem."

"Where's Honeyboy?" Robert Johnson called.

"Over here," Honeyboy Edwards said.

"Where's Honeyboy?"

"I'm over here, man."

"Honeyboy, where's Honeyboy gone off to?"

"He's over in the bafroom pullin' on his dick."

Robert Johnson cupped his hands and shouted, "Honeyboy? You playing with yourself again?"

"Fuck you," Honeyboy Edwards said. He got up from his bed and everyone started laughing.

Elvis Presley motioned everyone over to Henry's bed. "C'mon!" He held up his hand for everyone to be quiet.

Henry looked at the boys surrounding his bed and told them he was Saint Augustine. They all looked at each other, then at Henry. Elvis said, "No way, man. You can't do that."

"You can't be a saint," Howlin' Wolf said. "You got to be somebody *famous*."

Henry said Saint Augustine was famous.

"Saints aren't allowed," Otis Redding said.

Henry asked why not.

"It's a sin, that's why," Otis Redding said.

"And besides, it's a *pussy* name," Sid Vicious said and started laughing.

"Hey! Shut up, man," Robert Johnson said. "That's *blast*phemy."

Sid Vicious made a face and stuck his tongue out and went back to his bed.

Henry said call me Barbelo, then.

"Who the fuck is that?" Howlin' Wolf asked.

"Never heard of him," Sid Vicious called over from his bed. "Is it a group?"

Barbelo is the first thought, the womb of everything, the mother/father, the first man, the Holy Spirit, the thrice male, the thrice powerful.

"Say *what?*" Howlin' Wolf said.

"You can't just make up any old name you want," Elvis Presley said.

"Yeah, you got to be somebody!" Howlin' Wolf said.

"How 'bout Queen," Kurt Cobain said. "You could be Queen. They're a band."

Everybody laughed and said, "Queen! That's it!"

"He can't be Queen," Jimi Hendrix said.

"That's right," Ernest Whiskey Red Brown said. "No way he can be Queen. Prince, maybe."

Everyone laughed.

Henry said Barbelo was the first thought that came forth from the invisible virginal spirit.

"Sure, man, whatever you say," Elvis Presley said. "It's just that you got to have a name that other people can *re-late* to."

Otis Redding pushed his way to the front of the group. "You 'member what we told you?"

Henry said nothing.

"Pick a name or we'll pick one for you, dipshit."

"Hey, Dipshit, I like that," Ernest Whiskey Red Brown said.

"He *picked* a name, man," Jimi Hendrix said.

"It can't be just any name he ever heard," Otis Redding said. "It has to be a *real* name."

"That's right, man," Honeyboy Edwards said. "We all *famous* here."

"That's right," Keith Moon said. "We don't want anyone hanging around who *isn't.*"

"Pick another name," Elvis Presley said.

"He *picked* a fuckin' name," Jimi Hendrix said.

Henry said Barbelo was the first thought, which was the thought of God.

"Gimme a fucking *break,* mate," Sid Vicious said. "You some kind of born-again Christian?"

"There ain't nothing wrong with being born again," Honeyboy Edwards said. "Robert Johnson got born again."

"He was a bluesman," Sid Vicious said.

"Where you think he got the blues *from?* Piece-of-shit punk," Honeyboy Edwards said.

Elmore James laughed.

"Kiss my ass! You piece of honky dogshit!" Honeyboy Edwards kissed his hand and slapped himself on the rear with it.

"Just shut the fuck up!" Jimi Hendrix said. "All of you."

"Okay, okay," Otis Redding said. "Name some Barbelo songs. If anyone ever heard of them, you can be Barbelo."

Henry said there were no songs, only some books that were found in a cave in Egypt.

"What the *fuck?*" Robert Johnson said. He clapped and spun around on one foot and John Lennon did it too.

"Yo, man, why you always copy everything Robert Johnson does?" Otis Redding asked John Lennon. "Names that come from books ain't allowed," he said. "They got to be *famous* names. How the fuck are we supposed to know someone's name who came out of a cave in Egypt?" He laughed and everybody started to laugh. "Yo, man," he shouted. "The kid wants to be a fucking Egyptian caveman."

"Is Barbelo a *brother*?" Honeyboy Edwards asked. "If the dude's from Egypt, then he's a *African*."

"That's right," Ernest Whiskey Red Brown said. "Has to be a famous *white* dude."

"That's right," Elvis Presley said. "When I got here I wanted to be Kokomo Arnold, but nobody let me. That's why I had to be Elvis Presley."

"I bet Elvis thought he was Kokomo Arnold too," Honeyboy said.

"You're being racist," Jimi Hendrix said.

"It ain't racist," Otis Redding said. "It's just the way it is."

"It's still racist," Jimi Hendrix said.

"You don't know what the fuck you talking 'bout," Otis Redding said. "Elvis *wanted* to be black. Ever'body knows that. Don't mean it can happen! Michael Jackson wants to be white. Don't mean it's gonna happen."

"It's racist!" Jimi Hendrix said.

Otis Redding got mad. "You too caught up in that sixties shit."

"Yeah, shut the fuck up," Honeyboy Edwards said. "Is Barbelo a brother? Or a white dude?"

Henry said he didn't know.

"Pick another name, man," Otis Redding said.

"He *picked* a fucking name," Jimi Hendrix said. He pushed his way out of the circle and went over to his bed. "Bunch of fucking idiots."

"No way Barbelo's famous if you don't even know what he *looked* like," Otis Redding said.

"That's right, man. You don't even know if he's black or white," Elvis Presley said.

"You got one more chance," Otis Redding said.

Just then Mr. Miller came in and called, "Lights out!"

When it was dark Elvis Presley said, "He wants to be a fucking Egyptian caveman." Everybody started laughing until Mr. Miller came in and warned them to cut it out.

The next morning while they were making their beds Robert Johnson said, "There's a band named the Egyptians."

"Yeah, I heard them on the radio," Ernest Whiskey Red Brown said. "The Egyptians!"

Otis Redding came over to Henry's bed. "Listen up, everybody." He pointed to Henry. "From now on you are the Egyptian."

Henry looked at all the boys standing over their beds and said I went into the realm of darkness and I endured until I entered the middle of the prison. And the darkness of chaos shook.

Otis Redding clapped Henry on the back and spun around on one foot. "The Egyptian. You one *baaaad* muhfucker, man!" Then he went back to finish making his bed.

In church the priests say, *Lamb of God who takes away the sins of the world, have mercy on us.* Once when Henry asked Father Crowley why lamb? Father Crowley said, "Because the Agnus Dei is the symbol of Christ, and lamb is the sacrificial animal slaughtered in ancient times to give praise to God. When Jesus died on the cross to save man from sin and redeem him into everlasting life with the Father, he was taking the place of the sacrificial lamb, and that is why we say the Agnus Dei during the mass."

At Saint Jude's they talked about God sending his son to die for the sins of the world, and Saint Augustine said Jesus Christ was both victor and victim and it was because he was the victim that he was also the victor. But Henry's angel said that Christ was sent to ransom, not to redeem, because the dead are the ransom paid by the living for the Creator's mistake. The angel said there are no sacrifices, there are only victims, and by playing the lamb Christ wasn't taking away the sins of the world, he was showing the only way out of it.

The same day that Henry became the Egyptian, Robert Johnson told the story about the man who lived in the woods, Hatchet Harry. He was a bank robber who drove a big black car and never stayed in one place for more than a night because the FBI was always right on his tail. One night he robbed a bank in Philly. He thought he made a clean getaway but suddenly he heard sirens behind him. He drove as fast as he could and cut through alleys and drove all over the place until he got onto a road leading out into the country. As he came around a curve he saw a big open gate and he turned into it. That was how he gave the cops the slip.

It was in the days when the old millionaire still lived in the mansion all alone. One night the old man was lying in his big bed. He heard a car pull up in the driveway and went to the window and saw a man get out and begin prowling around. He went down to the room where he kept his collection of old swords and armor and he grabbed a battle-ax, the kind that is curved and sharp on both sides. The gangster prowled around and looked into all the rooms. Then, just as he came into the dining room, the old millionaire stepped out from behind the door and buried the axe in the man's head.

"AAAHHHHHHHHHHHH," Robert Johnson screamed. Everyone in the dining room stopped talking. Robert Johnson drew a line with his fork from the middle of his forehead down to the bridge of his nose and got spaghetti sauce in his hair.

"Let's try to keep the noise to a minimum," Mr. Miller called from his table near the window. "And cut the clowning," he said to Robert Johnson.

"Muhfucker never died," Robert Johnson whispered. "The axe was so fuckin' sharp it stayed there in his skull and not even one drop of blood came out. Muhfucker ran 'round screamin' and screamin', then he started laughing 'cause he couldn't believe he was still fuckin' alive and also 'cause the ax went into his brain and made him crazy." He picked up a handful of spaghetti from his plate. "This is what his brains looked like." He squished the spaghetti through his fingers. "He ran out of the mansion into the woods and only a couple of people ever seen him since. Sometimes late at night you can hear him laughing." Then he made a high-pitched, screeching laugh, "HEEEE HE HE HE HE."

Later Henry asked Mr. Miller if the story about Hatchet Harry was true.

Mr. Miller laughed. "It's an old tradition around here," he said. "In my day there were two versions. One about Hatchet Harry, who was a gangster, and another was Meat Cleaver Mulligan. He was a butcher. His shop in town was attacked and he was killed by an angry mob during the cholera epidemic of 1859."

Henry asked why.

"Because they thought he was spreading the disease by selling bad meat."

Henry asked if it was true.

"I suppose cholera could be spread that way—but I'm not positive."

Henry said no, he meant which *story* was true.

"It depends on who is telling it."

Henry said then it was sort of like the Gospels.

"How do you figure that?"

Henry said they all told the same story in different ways and so they were all true in their own way and that meant the stories were true in more ways than one.

"I'll have to think about that," Mr. Miller said. "But right off the top of my head, I'd say there is a huge difference between the story of Hatchet Harry and the New Testament."

Sy's sister and Helena were both sitting down when Henry came into the visiting room. Helena was holding a baby. Sy's sister jumped up and hugged Henry with both arms and rocked from side to side so that it was hard for him to breathe. "Oh, Henry, it's so good to see you. Are you okay?" Then she let him go and took his hand and pulled him over to where Helena was sitting with the baby in her lap.

Helena pulled the blanket away so Henry could see the baby's face. She looked different than Henry remembered but it was a combination of older and younger and happier and sadder. Henry bent down for a closer look and the baby burped. "He just ate," Helena said.

Henry asked what his name was.

"Ali," Helena said.

Just like his father, Henry said.

"That's right," Helena said. "His full name is Ali ben-Mohammed Ali. It means Ali, son of Mohammed Ali."

"But I just call him Al," Sy's sister said and touched the baby's nose.

The baby looked up at Helena and she bent down and kissed it and made a motherly noise. "What do you think, Henry?"

Henry asked why the top of its head was throbbing.

"That's the baby's fontanel."

Henry asked what that was.

"It's the soft spot on a baby's skull." She touched it lightly with her hand.

Henry looked at the baby and watched the spot on its head pulse. Then he said the children a woman bears resemble that man who loves her.

"He does look a lot like his father," Helena said.

"He has his father's forehead, but he's all mom around the mouth and eyes," Sy's sister said.

Helena lifted the baby up onto her shoulder and began to pat it on the back. "He has gas," she said.

"All babies have gas," Sy's sister said. Then she told Henry to sit down and tell them how he was doing.

"We wanted to come visit you sooner," Helena said. "But something came up."

"That's one way of putting it," Sy's sister said. She laughed. It sounded a little like Big Henry's laugh and just as Henry was about to ask about him she reached into her bag and took out a book. "This is a present from Big Henry," she said.

It was *The Baseball Book of Records*. Henry opened it and leafed through the pages. He remembered the way Big Henry talked and wondered if this was the book he had learned to talk that way from. He remembered the time Big Henry took him to the Hippodrome in Philadelphia and had four hot dogs, two bags of popcorn, and seven beers. He asked Sy's sister if she was still angry at him.

"I married him," she laughed. "So I guess you could say I'll *always* be angry at him."

Henry asked why she married Big Henry if she'd always be angry at him.

She pulled Henry to her and messed up his hair. "It was just a joke, Henry. Why do you take everything so *seriously?*"

Henry asked how far away Philadelphia was.

Sy's sister looked at Helena. "It's a long way away," she said. "A long, long, long way away."

Henry asked if they knew where his father was.

Sy's sister shook her head.

Henry asked Helena if she knew where her mother and Sy were.

Helena shook her head and then bent down and nuzzled the baby as if she had hardly heard what Henry had asked.

He asked if they were ever coming back.

Sy's sister pulled Henry up close and said, "Try not to think about it too much, okay, Henry? Let's just say they're underground."

Henry remembered what the emperor had said and asked if his father had a new job at the Palace.

"Not likely," Sy's sister said.

He asked if they were dead.

Sy's sister held him by the shoulders and looked at him for a long time. "These are questions that you'll have to save for later, Henry. Much later. For now, you should try not to think too much about it."

They were all quiet for a while. Then Helena said, "Saint Jude's is a really nice place, Henry."

Henry said the strong who are held in high regard are great people and the weak who are despised are the obscure.

Helena put the baby back down on her lap. "What's that mean?" she asked.

"You don't have to explain," Sy's sister said. "I heard you loud and clear." She put a hand on his shoulder. "Try not to be sad, Henry. We are all very proud of you."

Helena tickled her baby under its chin and it began to make a gurgling sound. Then she unbuttoned the front of her blouse and lifted out one of her breasts. She guided the nipple into the baby's mouth. Henry tried not to look but he couldn't help seeing that her nipple was big and brown. She held it between her fingers the way people held cigarettes. When the baby was attached she looked up.

Helena and Sy's sister stayed until the baby finished eating. Then they both hugged and kissed Henry and told him that they would come back again to visit him soon. When they were gone Henry went outside to look for Mr. Miller. He found him at the basketball court watching Otis Redding and Jim Morrison playing one-on-one. Mr. Miller was wearing high-tops, which meant he was going to play the winner. Henry gave Mr. Miller *The Baseball Book of Records* because personal property wasn't allowed at Saint Jude's.

Mr. Miller looked at the book. "Thanks, Henry. We'll put it in the library and you can look at it anytime you want to."

Then Henry said he didn't want to see any more visitors.

Mr. Miller closed the book. "What do you mean, Henry?"

Henry said he didn't want to see anyone else who came to see him.

"What happened?" Mr. Miller put a hand on Henry's shoulder. "Are you okay?"

Henry watched Jim Morrison do a layup.

"C'mon," Mr. Miller said. "Let's play some ball."

Later Henry was raking leaves outside the dorm. His team was assigned to yard detail. When a team was assigned a place to work Mr. Miller got out an old army hat and wrote each job on a piece of paper and the members of the team drew to see what job they got. Henry got raking.

Mr. Miller stood behind Henry and watched him rake. He was always standing around and asking questions or telling everyone what to do or asking if he could play too. Henry had heard Howlin' Wolf say Mr. Miller was a loser

because anyone who came back to Saint Jude's after getting out had to be. He didn't even have a car and had to
take the bus when he got his day off.

"Good job, Henry," Mr. Miller said.

Henry didn't look up or say anything but just kept
making long swipes with the rake that sent the leaves flying behind him. He was trying to imagine how anything
could shed so much of itself and still be the same thing afterward. He asked Mr. Miller if trees died when they
dropped their leaves and then came back to life, or if they
stayed alive all winter without them.

"Good question, Henry. They stay alive but go dor-
mant, sort of like animals that hibernate."

Henry raked and said nothing.

"Mind if I ask you a question, Henry?"

Henry kept raking.

"Why'd you let that gorilla out of the cage?"

Henry backed into the pile of leaves behind him and
stood in it and kept raking. He didn't want to talk about
Big Nekkid. At night sometimes Henry thought about Big
Nekkid. He was sorry Big Nekkid had been killed. But he
wasn't sorry he had freed her. Freeing Big Nekkid had been
a good deed, like the story Father John had told the other
day about Jesus bringing Lazarus back from the dead. Letting Big Nekkid go was like releasing her from captivity
and saints knew a lot about captivity because they were
captives too. They were captives of their sainthood and

that meant they didn't have any choice but to do good deeds. They were called to them.

Mr. Miller moved out of the way of the flying leaves. "Why'd you do it, Henry?"

Henry said because he had to.

"You had to?"

Henry said he wanted to too.

"Are you sorry?"

Henry said nothing.

"I have to know, Henry," Mr. Miller said. He stood at the edge of Henry's leaf pile. "I'm trying to help."

Henry raked.

"Just tell me you're sorry. Are you?"

Henry said no. He stopped raking and looked around at the job he'd done. The raked grass looked like a big scar.

"Would you explain why you're not sorry?"

Henry said because he wasn't.

"Even though what you did led to the death of an innocent animal? How can you say you're not sorry for what you did?"

Henry said why should he be? Jesus wasn't sorry for raising Lazarus up from the dead.

"Henry, drop the rake. I want you to explain."

Henry asked if bringing someone back to life was a good deed.

"It wasn't just a good deed, Henry. It was a miracle."

Henry said well, Jesus didn't say he was sorry.

"What are you talking about?"

Lazarus was four days in the tomb. Did Jesus say he was sorry when Lazarus died a second time *all over again?*

Mr. Miller just stood there for a minute. "Don't forget to do under the bushes," he said and walked across the newly raked lawn toward the rectory.

Henry sat in Father Rogan's office listening to the two priests talk.

"It's just a routine procedure," Father Rogan said. "Custody has to be worked out in court. But if they start anything fancy or try to impugn the reputation of this institution, I'll wash my hands of the whole thing."

Father Crowley said, "Of course. I agree with you completely." Then he turned to Henry. "I hear you had some visitors yesterday! How did it go?"

Henry said fine.

Father Crowley arched his eyebrows as if he didn't believe him. "We can talk about it later."

"Father Crowley has managed to find you a benefactor, son," Father Rogan said. He crossed his arms and clasped his elbows and leaned forward so his bald head and shoulders became like a shadow cast across the desk.

"Do you remember Mrs. Fontane?" Father Crowley asked. "We visited her in the hospital. Remember?"

Henry nodded.

"Well, Mrs. Fontane has offered to sponsor you here at Saint Jude's, and Father Rogan has agreed to accept that arrangement. It means you can stay here as a regular student."

Father Rogan nodded his head. "It's not the way we usually do things." He leaned back in his chair. "But I have decided to make an exception in your case."

"There are still some things that need to be ironed out," Father Crowley said. "But don't worry. Between Father Rogan and myself, you have some pretty solid support." Then he leaned toward Henry. "You don't look too happy, Henry. Is there something you'd like to say?"

Henry said he wanted his books back.

"Is that all you can think of? Do you have any idea of the time and the effort that the people have been expending on your behalf?"

Henry said they are lowly indeed compared to the perfect glory.

"The rules that apply to the others also apply to you," Father Rogan said. "No personal property of any kind is permitted. Everyone shares alike, and nobody does without."

"Tomorrow afternoon some people are coming to interview you," Father Crowley said. "Their decision will depend on how well you cooperate."

"That is exactly correct," Father Rogan said. "Ask the Lord for guidance."

Father Crowley nodded in agreement. "And hold your tongue, son. Don't try to be smart. It'll only spoil things."

"That's enough for now," Father Rogan said. "Run along. We have other business to discuss."

Father Crowley made the sign of the cross over Henry and squeezed his shoulder. "That's a good boy, Henry."

On Fridays after dinner Saint Jude's divided up into two teams that were like the factions in the Hippodrome except they weren't called Blues and Greens, they were the Reds and the Whites. Instead of fighting about whether Jesus was human and divine or just divine or just human, they killed each other trying to capture the other team's flag. Each team had a general and everyone wore a colored strip of cloth around his waist. You killed someone by pulling off his flag. When you were killed you were out of the game and had to go straight to the front steps of the chapel and stay there until the game was over. You weren't allowed to say anything to anyone on the way even if you had been carrying the flag when you were killed. If you were carrying the other team's flag when you were killed the person who killed you got the flag and it was their problem after that. The whole point of the game was to get the other team's flag and deliver it to your general. Anyone caught fighting or doing anything stupid or dangerous—like climbing onto the roof of the dorm or hiding in one of the walk-in freezers in the kitchen—was thrown out of the game. It was the general's job to make up the strategy. You had to obey his orders and if he suspected you of collaboration with the enemy he could have you shot.

Otis Redding explained these rules to Henry on their way to meet the rest of the Red team. The dorm groups were mostly kept together but a few from their section played with the Whites. It was so the sides were even. There were seventy-four boys at Saint Jude's so each team had thirty-seven players. Keith Moon and Elmore James played for the Whites. Otis Redding said it was okay because they weren't such good players anyway. He said the best players were the crazy ones who would do crazy things. Field Marshal Rommel was the craziest and that's why he was always chosen to be the Red general. The general for the Whites was Attila the Hun. He was crazy too but not as crazy as Rommel. The last two games had ended without any winner and when they got to their fort behind the gym Field Marshal Rommel was explaining the new strategy to everybody. "We're going to use guerrilla tactics," he said. "That should confuse the fuck out of them. If we can't get the flag, at least we can wipe them out."

"The rules are that if nobody gets the flag, then it's a tie," Jimi Hendrix said.

"Well, I say if we kill them all, we win," Rommel said. "Fuck the flag."

"But that's not the point of the game."

Rommel spat on the ground. "The way I see it, if we kill them all, it's the same as winning. Ever hear of *total war?*"

Field Marshal Rommel suddenly seemed as dangerous to Henry as Mr. Earl. He didn't want to play. He tried to move out of the circle but just then the belts with the red flags came around. Otis Redding showed Henry how to tie the belt around his waist in a way that made it harder for the enemy to kill him. "Even though it's called capture the flag," he said, "the funnest part about it is trying to stay alive until the end." He yanked Henry's flag off his belt and held it up. "Getting killed is as easy as that. And once you're dead, the fun's over."

Rommel told everyone to shut up. He looked at his field watch. "Seventeen minutes to get into position," he said.

Otis Redding opened his hand and showed Henry a plug of chewing tobacco. He took it between two fingers and shoved it way back into his cheek. "You better keep quiet, dude. I'll know who told if I get caught." He smiled and it looked like he had an infected tooth.

"Paint up," Rommel said. A couple of guys with burnt corks went around making everybody's face black. Otis Redding and some other guys took out red lipstick and went around making war marks on everyone's face. Then Rommel pointed out across the lawn and spat some tobacco onto the ground. "Let's waste 'em, dudes."

Otis Redding spat too and turned to Henry. "C'mon!" he said and tore off into the woods.

There were no sieges and besieged or advances and retreats or emissaries and ambassadors or standoffs or lines in the sand or prisoners of war or forced marches. There was only in-bounds and out-of-bounds. Henry was put into a group of skirmishers. Their mission was to comb through the woods and engage the enemy whenever they found him and to make as much noise as possible when they got into a fight. As soon as they reached the woods the war began. Henry hid behind a tree and felt a flush of animal vigor overcome him. He was frightened for his life and at the same time he felt exhilarated at the possibility that he might lose it at any moment. The angel in his ear said something about fear underlying both the noblest and the most evil deeds of men, but he didn't hear exactly because his heart was beating hard and blood was heating up his ears.

Henry watched the way the other skirmishers ran from tree to tree and dove behind bushes and fallen logs. He stayed behind his tree and waited. He could hear voices and see shadows and shapes moving about. A great racket erupted from the direction of the dormitory and Henry saw three Whites chasing a Red across the lawn. They were yelling and their flags were streaming behind them. The Red they were chasing was John Lennon. He was shrieking but Henry couldn't make out what he was trying to say and when they disappeared around the corner of the dorm there was a loud bang that sounded like the side door to the building slamming.

Henry wanted to move but he didn't know where to go. He wanted to spy on the battle from a safe place. His angel said without fear you are plunged deeper into darkness. To be without fear is to be without knowledge and only by knowledge can you enter the light.

Somebody went *psst* and Henry looked but he didn't see anybody. The person went *psst* again. It was Pigpen. He was squatting behind a bush about twenty feet from Henry. He pressed his finger to his lips and made a motion with his hand that meant Henry should stay where he was and be quiet. Then he pointed in the direction of a big pine tree. There was a White standing next to it. Henry guessed he was a sapper, which meant his job was to roam around looking for groups of Reds and when he saw them to sneak up and try to kill one—even if that meant sacrificing himself. A sapper's job was only to harass.

Pigpen raced to another tree and another and another until he was practically next to the enemy. The White didn't move but just kept standing there like he was waiting for somebody. Suddenly Pigpen pounced. The White let out a yell and Pigpen tackled him. There was a flurry of hands and legs as each tried to kill the other. Then Pigpen stood up holding the flag he'd pulled and waved it over his head and in the face of his victim. Suddenly three Whites sprang out. Before Pigpen could even yell they had him down and pulled his flag. They let out a war cry that echoed through the woods and disappeared into the trees again.

Henry didn't move. Pigpen and the White he'd killed both started off toward the front steps of the chapel, where the dead gathered. They didn't look in Henry's direction. The rules were that you weren't allowed to interfere in the game after you got killed. The dead weren't allowed to acknowledge the living and the living weren't allowed to acknowledge the dead. They were out of the game for good.

Henry sat on the ground and leaned against the tree. The sun was setting and the shadows in the woods went from long to nothing. From where he sat on the ground, Henry could look up into the treetops and see the gathering blackness. The lights were coming on in the rectory and the other buildings. Fear closed around Henry and beat around his ears and muffled his thoughts. He didn't know if he should keep moving or stay put to avoid getting killed. The angel in his ear repeated the part about light and fear and knowledge but Henry's fear stayed and he slouched lower to the ground.

A group of Whites burst from the woods and began to race across the lawn. They were followed by a group of Reds led by Elvis Presley, who was shouting and waving the flags of the Whites he'd killed. The Whites began to scatter in different directions. One by one they were brought down, and it was impossible to separate the howls of the victors from the laughing shrieks of the vanquished.

Then it was over. The Reds, led by Elvis Presley, reassembled and began to return to the woods. The dead got up and brushed themselves off and made for the chapel steps. They talked among themselves and one or two swore loudly and flipped the bird at the Reds, who were tucking their trophies into their pockets. Then Mr. Miller appeared with his whistle around his neck. The dead gathered around him and some pointed into the woods. Henry couldn't hear what they were telling him. Mr. Miller listened for a minute, nodding, then he sent the dead on their way and jogged off in the other direction.

Henry was suddenly ashamed. Saints don't cling to the forest floor in fear. They walk through the forest and talk to all the creatures that live there. He stood up and brushed himself off and glanced around. Then he began walking. But before he reached the edge of the woods he was brought down by three Whites. One had him by the neck, another knocked his legs out from underneath him, and the third yanked the flag from his belt and did a jig while waving it in Henry's face.

Henry said let me up.

"You're dead, man."

Henry said let me go.

"We killed you, dude."

Henry said I'm not dead.

"Like shit you're not!"

Henry said it's only a game and I quit.

The boys looked at each other and then at Henry. "We'll show you a game you can't quit, fuckhead." They pulled Henry up and twisted his arm behind his back and pushed him farther into the woods. "Only babies quit," the boy with the flag said.

Henry said let me go.

"Shut up. You're a prisoner."

Henry said prisoners aren't allowed.

"You're a dead prisoner, dude." The boys laughed and one of them whacked Henry on the head with the flag. "What's your dorm team?"

Henry said nothing.

"You're in Mr. Willis's class."

Henry said nothing.

"Wussy Willis."

"Pussy Willis."

Then they pushed Henry onto the ground. The three boys stood over him. "Let's strip him," someone said. They began pulling off Henry's pants. Henry kicked and yelled for them to stop. One boy's nose began to bleed. "That's it, fucker! You die!" He kicked back and Henry's nose began to bleed too. Then when Henry was naked they took their flags and bound Henry's hands behind his back and his feet and bound his knees and left his clothes in a pile next to him.

"That's for when Hatchet Harry finds you."

"See you later, sucker!"

Then they all disappeared into the woods laughing the Hatchet Harry laugh. There was blood all over Henry's chin and in his mouth. He rolled onto his stomach. The dirt stuck to his face where the tears rolled. His angel cried out, Henry is one of your creatures, Lord! His instinct is to know you. He bears about him the mark of death to remind him that you abandoned him. Still, he wishes to know you. He cannot be content unless he knows you. You made him for yourself, and his heart will find no peace until he finds you. Then the angel fell silent and Henry began to shiver because it was cold.

ATLANTIC CITY

Henry was called into Father Rogan's office the next morning. "Are you feeling better?" Father Rogan asked.

Henry nodded.

"Pretty tender, huh?" Father Rogan touched his fingertips to the blue swelling on Henry's cheek. He sat down behind his desk. "Until you tell me who did this, I'm holding everyone responsible. That means I'm cutting free time until the end of the year, and no more capture the flag. Do you think that's fair?"

Henry said nothing.

"By protecting those boys, you're punishing the rest. Is that what you want?"

Henry said nothing.

"Think about it," Father Rogan said. Then he got up and opened the door.

Farley the policewoman came in with two other people. One was a social worker and the other was from the adoption agency. They looked at Henry while Father Rogan said some things and one of them wrote in a pad.

"Looks like you got hit pretty hard, Henry." Farley bent down and looked at Henry closely. She still smelled like cough medicine and the ring on her finger still looked too tight.

The social worker bent down and asked some questions but Henry didn't answer. Father Crowley had told him to hold his tongue.

"Can you tell us what happened?" Farley asked.

"Some of the older boys got rough with him," the priest said. "We're still trying to straighten it out."

The man from the adoption agency asked Henry some questions. He repeated every question twice but Henry didn't answer. "It looks to me like the boy's been traumatized," the man said to Father Rogan.

Father Rogan frowned. "It looks worse than it is," he said.

The man from the agency nodded and made notes. Then he opened up his briefcase and took out some papers. "Adoption papers have been filed," he said and he gave them to Father Rogan to look over.

Everything came down to questions after that. There were questions about Henry's current status and his previous status and his background and his condition and his prospects and his interests. "Answering the questions is not just a matter of record," Farley said. "It is of real concern to everybody."

Mr. Miller knew all about depositions and status and parental-rights termination because he said he had been through it all himself. He took Henry on a walk around the campus and told him a little about all the things that had happened to him when he was a boy. While Mr. Miller talked, Henry listened to the angel in his ear. The angel said there was a householder who had every conceivable thing, be it son or slave or cattle or dog or pig or corn or barley or chaff or grass or meat or acorn. He was a sensible fellow and he knew what the food of each one was.

Henry asked Mr. Miller if he had a dog.

"Nope. Never had a dog."

Henry asked Mr. Miller if he ever had a pig.

Mr. Miller stopped walking. "Have you been listening to any of what I've been saying?"

They were in front of the chapel, where the dead had gathered the night before. After the game, when Mr. Miller realized Henry was missing, he had led a group of boys from the dorm into the woods with his flashlight. Henry could hear them calling his name but he didn't answer. Henry watched Mr. Miller's flashlight beam cut through the darkness and when it finally landed on him Henry didn't look up into it. He lay on his side and shivered while the angel in his ear said love your brother like your soul. Guard him like the pupil of your eye.

"Let's sit down," Mr. Miller said. They sat down on the steps of the chapel. Henry watched some boys throwing a Frisbee on the lawn. On Saturdays it was free time all day and you were allowed to do anything you wanted. You could check out equipment from the gym as long as you weren't on probation. If you were on probation you couldn't check things out unless you asked special permission first. Probation could last for a day or a week or a month at Saint Jude's, but Henry's angel told him that real probation lasted a lifetime.

"Can we get serious now?"

Henry said nothing.

"There are things in motion that have a lot to do with determining your future."

Henry asked Mr. Miller what he wanted.

"I want you to be straight with me."

Henry said nothing.

"You could have answered some of the questions they asked you in Father Rogan's office. They left with a bad impression because you wouldn't answer any questions."

Henry said he'd never had a dog or a pig.

Mr. Miller folded his arms across his knees and dropped his head onto them. "Give me a break, Henry. Please?"

Henry said if *he* had a dog or a pig, guess what he'd feed them?

Mr. Miller sighed. "I give up, Henry; what would you feed them?"

Henry said he would feed them nothing.

Mr. Miller lifted his head from his arms and watched the boys playing Frisbee for a few minutes.

Henry said he'd let them feed from the crumbs that fell from the table because everyone got the lot that fell to them.

"You're making a big mistake, Henry."

The Frisbee landed at their feet and Mr. Miller picked it up and threw it and it sailed over the heads of all the boys and landed at the edge of the woods. Then the chapel bell rang once, which meant it was time to go to lunch. "Any more nosebleeds?" Mr. Miller asked.

Henry shook his head.

"I don't blame you for being angry, Henry. But you should try not to let it prevent you from doing what's right. I have a pretty good idea who it was, so even if you don't cooperate, I'll get the truth one way or another."

Henry said names did not bring truth but truth brought names into existence.

"What are you saying, Henry?"

Henry said nothing.

"All I want is the names of the boys who beat you up," Mr. Miller said and stood up. "If you don't want help from anyone, just keep it up." He brushed his pants off and went to lunch.

In the lunchroom Father Rogan announced that free time was being cut by ten minutes and capture the flag was suspended until the boys responsible for beating up Henry stepped forward.

"That's not fair," Field Marshal Rommel said. He looked around the room as if he were talking for everybody.

"I'm the one who decides what's fair," Father Rogan said. "If I hear reports of any more fighting there will be serious consequences."

Everyone snuck glances at Henry but nobody spoke to him. He was hidden from the living in the tomb of his thoughts, and everyone was mad at him for spoiling their fun.

Henry peeked into Father Rogan's office. Father Crowley and Dr. Alt were both there. "Separation of church and state is one thing, but this is absurd," Father Rogan was saying.

"I'm meeting with the cardinal," Father Crowley said. Then he noticed Henry peeping in the door. "Stop spying and come in, Henry."

When he came into the room Dr. Alt beckoned to him. He touched the purple-and-yellow bruise on Henry's cheek. Father Crowley leaned forward for a look. "Has he been seen by a doctor?"

"The nurse will be in on Monday. Henry will get a thorough looking-over."

"What if something's broken?"

"I've seen enough scrapes and bruises to know what he needs. I'm running a home for boys, remember?"

"Would you like some time alone?" Father Crowley asked.

Dr. Alt shook his head. "I thought it might be nice if we all talked together. What do you think, Henry?"

Henry shrugged.

"Has your angel talked to you lately?"

Henry nodded and looked sideways at the two other priests, who were sitting with their legs crossed. Father Rogan had his elbows on the arms of his chair and was making a tent with his fingers.

"What has the angel said?"

Henry said stuff.

"What kind of stuff?"

Henry said just stuff.

"What's the last thing the angel said to you? Think hard. I want to know exactly."

Henry said it is always a matter of the will, not the act.

The other priests were listening with eager looks on their faces. "What do you think the angel meant by that?" Dr. Alt asked.

Henry said it depended.

"What does it depend on?"

Henry said it depended on whether you had been res-urrected.

Dr. Alt was quiet for a minute. He looked at the ground, not at the other priests. "Could you explain it a little more?"

Henry said those who say they will die first and then rise are in error. If they do not first receive the resurrection while they live, then when they die they will receive nothing.

"Did the angel tell you that too?"

Henry nodded.

"What do you think the angel was trying to tell you?"

Henry shrugged.

"What were you doing when the angel spoke?"

Henry said playing capture the flag.

"Did the angel speak before or after the boys beat you up?"

Henry said before.

"Interesting," the old priest said.

"I don't think so at all," Father Rogan interrupted.

"Why not?" the old priest asked.

Father Rogan dropped his hands into his lap. "I've been around boys long enough to know when they're playing games. Henry is leading us around by the nose. He's been doing it from the beginning."

Dr. Alt straightened up in his seat. "How do you suppose that?"

"You know as well as I do, Father. You know full well that the boy is merely repeating things he has read."

"That may be the case," the old priest said. "But the interesting thing is not *where* the words come from. It's the spontaneity of his utterances."

"Rubbish. There is nothing mysterious about any of it. The boy is merely parroting."

"You mean to say that you don't find his statements interesting or revealing?"

"Look, nobody doubts that the boy has a photographic memory. I'm as impressed by that as anyone. It's remarkable. But he's obviously unable to comprehend any of what he says. Why, he just said so himself."

"He did?"

"You heard it. Didn't he just say, 'It is always a matter of the will, not the act'?"

The old doctor smiled and nodded. He rubbed his chin but didn't say anything.

"It's all haphazard, nothing more," Father Rogan said.

Father Crowley cleared his throat. "Father Rogan has a very good point." He cleared his throat again. "I've been doing some interesting reading lately. I find myself agreeing with William James on certain things."

"What does William James have to do with anything?" Father Rogan cut in.

"Well, not a lot, I suppose. Just something I noticed in my reading. Made me think that maybe we should look at the way Henry's particularities work as a whole."

"Precisely," Father Rogan said. "And taken as a whole, all I see is one mischievous little boy leading us all around by the nose."

"Fine. But even if you're entirely correct, you're still left with plenty to explain," Father Crowley said. "We should concentrate on the pragmatics of it, use a sort of Jamesian approach."

"And what, exactly, does that mean?"

"Well, for one thing, it means looking into the sources of the boy's inspiration. As well as the contents of his statements and the objects of his intentions. Everything taken as a whole."

Father Rogan stood up and waved his arm. "You're taking it all too seriously. Both of you."

Father Crowley's face got red. "If you'll allow me to continue. To quote James, it means reading in *common matters superior expressions of meaning*. I was quite taken by that line, Father. Are you going to accuse me of haphazard recapitulation?"

"Come, come now," the old priest cut in. "We're not here to argue."

"That's right," Father Rogan said. "I have a school to run, and it's boys like Henry that make my job difficult enough. I don't have time to ponder the objects of their intentions or the sources of their inspiration on top of all the baggage they arrive on my doorstep with." Then he went over to his desk and sat down and put on his reading glasses and started looking at papers.

Henry watched Father Rogan sorting through the pile on his desk. Then he said the resurrection is not a matter of the act. To receive it in this life is a matter of the will.

"Hmmmm," Father Rogan said and went back to sorting though his papers.

Father Crowley began to say something but Dr. Alt held up a hand. "Now is not the time for this discussion." He turned to Henry. "Why do you think your angel isn't trying to tell you anything?"

Father Rogan looked up and let the paper fall to his desk. "Maybe because it isn't."

"You don't think your angel is trying to say something to you? To communicate?" Dr. Alt asked Henry again.

Father Rogan stood up and leaned on his desk with both hands. "I think I've heard enough," he said. "Why don't we just take the boy at his word and drop the intellectualizing? We have more urgent business."

"What business is that?" Dr. Alt asked.

"The visit we will soon be paying to court, for starters. Or maybe you've forgotten."

"We are right on course, Father. I'm simply preparing for the testimony I've been asked to make."

"All they want to know is your opinion of the boy's emotional state, Father. Whether you think it important that he remain here, at Saint Jude's. They're not interested in a long discussion of psychoanalytic practice." He crossed his arms over his chest. "Do you know about his collection of books?"

"I do indeed," Dr. Alt said. "I know very well about them."

"Then I don't understand why it is so hard for you to accept that the boy is merely regurgitating. He's too young to understand what he's saying."

"Not only am I able to *accept* that," Dr. Alt said, "I'm prepared to go quite a bit further."

"Very good," Father Rogan said. "Could we get on with it, then?"

"If you'll indulge me for a moment," Dr. Alt said and held up his hand again. "What Henry is regurgitating are the esoteric writings of a gnostic community that flourished in the second and third centuries in Egypt. The recent discovery of these texts points to an interesting paradox. As you know, despite hermeneutical and other critical tools, such writings are exceedingly difficult to interpret. On top of that, it is the *nature* of esoteric writings to be incomprehensible to everyone except those who have been initiated into their secrets." He crossed his legs and rubbed his kneecap and smiled a knowing smile. "Jung was, as you probably know, very interested in the gnostics."

"Why bring Jung into it?" Father Rogan said. "Or any brand of psychology, for that matter?"

"Because we live in an age of psychology, and today experience is formulated in those terms. We possess a different vocabulary and are working with completely different precepts than the authors of these ancient writings. Jung took a great interest in gnosticism, provided valuable interpretative tools. We must not let our prejudices blind us to opportunities that present themselves—however strange they may seem at first. You see, Father, not only do I think *Henry* is unable to understand them; at present I don't think *any* of us can."

Father Rogan looked at Father Crowley and Henry and then turned back to Dr. Alt. He ran his hand back and forth over his bald head as if he were shining it. "I don't see how this has anything to do with anything."

"I'm a little puzzled too," Father Crowley agreed.

"I'm sorry. All I mean to say is that you are merely stating the obvious when you say Henry is regurgitating. He is doing *exactly* that. Regurgitation is the only way to recover what has been lost inside us. But it is a process of *returning*—returning, as a whirlpool returns in on itself, engulfs itself, swallows itself. Its symbol is the Uroboros."

"Uroboros?"

"The snake that devours its own tail. It is a perpetual act of recovery and return. The material that is being recovered and returned is the texts that the boy is regurgitating."

Father Rogan rolled his eyes. "I'm sorry I asked."

Dr. Alt patted Henry's knee. "I've been consulting on Henry's case with an old friend, an expert on the gnostics. He believes there are all sorts of implications."

"The only implications that concern me are what is going to happen when we get into court."

Father Crowley nodded. "I agree. But I also think it is important for Dr. Alt to pursue his investigations."

Father Rogan put on his reading glasses. "I think you're both making a mountain out of a molehill. It's the same old story. A child gets paraded around and all the latest theories get trotted out until the novelty wears off and everybody realizes that their expectations have been exaggerated. They return to their articles and their seminars. And where does the child end up?" He took off his reading glasses and fixed a stern look on his fellow priests. "In the end you're left with a few highly developed but debatable insights into the human psyche or gnosticism or piano playing or long division or what have you—and one confused and very unhappy child."

Father Crowley crossed his legs and cracked his ankle. Dr. Alt pulled out his handkerchief and began to clean his glasses.

"If it were up to me," Father Rogan said, "I'd take the religion out of psychology and the psychology out of religion altogether."

Dr. Alt put his glasses back. "You are oversimplifying."

"Maybe a little simplification is exactly what's needed."

"Let's not argue," Father Crowley said.

"Perhaps it would be better if Henry and I spoke alone after all," Dr. Alt said. "I didn't come to debate or have an argument. I only wanted to speak openly so that Henry feels he has all of our support and guidance. As to your critique of psychology and religion, I can only restate what my mentor once stated."

"And what is that?" Father Rogan asked.

"That symbols are the essence both of the psyche and of religious experience, and in understanding *symbols* we comprehend our *selves*." He picked up his cane from beside the chair with an old-man grunt and tapped it on the floor.

Father Rogan stood up. "You may go now, Henry," he said.

Henry got up and Father Crowley reached out and took his arm and pulled him closer. He looked at Henry's bruised eye. "I really do think it should be looked at right away."

"It can wait until Monday," Father Rogan replied. Then he nodded at Henry and told him to say good-bye to their guests.

Henry and the three priests drove together to Philadelphia. To get to Philadelphia you could go along the coast or on the inland road. If you went along the coast you passed through Prusa and Pergamum and Smyrna and Sardis but if you didn't want to go through those cities you could take a ship and get off at Ephesus and from there it took only a day. It was too early in the morning for breakfast so Father Rogan gave Henry a sandwich wrapped in plastic. Nobody talked much and Henry watched out the window. After a while he fell asleep.

When he woke up they were at the courthouse. Henry followed the three priests inside. They were like angels dressed all in black, one old and crabbed and two not so old. Father Rogan asked a guard for directions and the guard took them to a big room called family court.

The room was full and the judge sat up front behind a big desk. He was dressed in black too but he didn't look like a priest or an angel. All you could see was his head and shoulders, which looked sort of like a small piece of fruit resting on a big pedestal. The seal of the State of Pennsylvania was on the wall behind him. There were flags too. When Henry and the three priests entered, the judge didn't even look up but went on talking to the people standing in front of his desk. A guard showed them where to sit. Then he went up to the front of the courtroom and gave the judge a piece of paper and Henry unwrapped his sandwich and began to eat it.

"Put that away," Father Rogan said. "You're not allowed to eat in court."

Henry wrapped the sandwich back up and held it in his lap. He looked around the room to see if there were any windows but there were none. There were only chairs and tables and doors. The lights in the ceiling made every surface reflect and there was a humming in the background like the humming in Henry's ear.

The judge drank a glass of water and then looked at his watch. Father Crowley and Father Rogan were whispering and Dr. Alt had his cane between his knees and his hands on top and his eyes closed.

Theodora was across the room. There was a man sitting next to her. She smiled and waved to Henry but Henry didn't wave back. Father Crowley leaned over to Father Rogan. "That's her lawyer," he whispered. Henry didn't want to look at Theodora but he couldn't help it. She was dressed all in blue and didn't look like Porphyrius the whale anymore but like a demon in human form. Henry was scared. He wondered why Theodora was there and if she had come to send him underground just like his father. He wondered if his father had enough water and food to stay underground for a long time. Being underground meant living farther from the light than any other fallen creature.

Then Farley and Shumacher came into the room. They were wearing their police uniforms and carrying papers under their arms. They sat down at the table next to the man with the briefcase. Farley opened up a folder and Shumacher folded his hands on the table and looked straight ahead.

"Who is the probation officer?" the judge asked.

Farley stood up. "I am, your honor."

"And the law guardian?"

"I just saw him in the hall, your honor," Farley said. Just then a man walked into the courtroom. He was young and had a mustache. "Excuse me, your honor," he said. He came over to Henry.

"You must be Henry," the man whispered and offered his hand.

Henry shook the man's hand.

"Mr. Downey is your court-appointed law guardian," Father Crowley said.

"Is the representative from social services present?" the judge asked.

"They're on the way, your honor." Mr. Downey opened his briefcase.

"Well, I can't wait any longer," the judge said and told Mr. Downey to proceed.

Mr. Downey took some papers up to the judge. They talked for a minute, then Mr. Downey went back to his seat.

"Has there been a hearing?" the judge asked Farley.

Farley stood up. "There are no charges being filed, your honor." Then she said something about parental-rights termination.

The judge held up a folder. "I have the paperwork right here." Farley took some more papers up to him and Mr. Downey looked at the papers in his briefcase as though he didn't care what anyone else in the room was doing. The man sitting next to Theodora did the same thing and Shumacher sat with his hands folded on the table and looked straight ahead. He had the same sore look on his face as when he told Henry that Big Nekkid was dead and it was all Henry's fault.

After a little while Farley went back and sat down. The judge shuffled papers, then he looked over to where Henry and the priests were sitting. Father Crowley smiled and nodded but he didn't say anything.

The judge lifted the stack of papers up and dropped them back down on his desk. "We have a lot of ground to cover," he said. "Is there a Father Rogan present?"

"Yes, your honor." Father Rogan stood up.

"You are aware that adoption procedures have been initiated, Father?" He nodded in the direction of Theodora and the man with the briefcase.

"I am, your honor," Father Rogan said.

"What grounds do you have for contesting the adoption?"

"The grounds that the boy's interests and needs would best be met at Saint Jude's. I believe that Henry should remain there."

The man with the briefcase stood up. "May I approach the bench?"

The judge nodded.

The man took up a pile of papers and they talked for a minute and the judge looked over at Theodora, who returned the judge's look with a sterner one, and then the man went back and sat down at his table. The judge looked at his watch. "We will adjourn until after lunch," he said.

A saint could be in different places at the same time without going anywhere. Saints brought their surroundings with them and that's why people called them holy. If it was raining outside a saint could walk around as if the sun were shining and if there were plagues and wars a saint went around as if they were nothing dangerous. If you didn't care it didn't matter, and it if didn't matter nothing bad could ever happen to you. Sometimes people got angry at saints. They stoned them and crucified them and cut their limbs off one by one and skinned them alive and boiled them and tried to get them to come down to earth. But saints were already down-to-earth and the only thing that made a saint a saint was that a saint knew it more fully and felt it more deeply than other people.

They were sitting at a table in the lunchroom. Henry ate his sandwich while the three priests and Mr. Downey talked about what they were going to do. Mr. Downey ate two hot dogs and drank a Diet Coke. He wasn't fat but he looked like he was. He sweated when he ate. The priests didn't eat because it was Lent and at Saint Jude's the priests ate only one meal a day during Lent.

"We're fighting a losing battle," Mr. Downey said. "The court almost always chooses a family situation over an institutional one."

"There is no way," Father Rogan said, "that a single woman who runs a casino can be considered a family situation."

"You may be right about that, Father," Mr. Downey said. "All I'm saying is that the court will choose a stable and responsible individual over an institution any day, especially if the individual is a woman with money and political influence."

"What about Mrs. Fontane?" Father Crowley asked. "She is willing to subsidize Henry's entire education. Why wouldn't that be enough?"

"It's a question of parental rights," Mr. Downey said. "If Mrs. Fontane were the legal guardian, she could send Henry to any school and pay for as much education as she wants. But she isn't."

The priests looked at Henry. "Still hungry?" Father Rogan asked.

Henry shook his head.

"In my opinion our time would have been better spent trying to persuade her privately," Mr. Downey said. "But it's too late for that."

Father Rogan didn't say anything. He looked into his glass of water and Henry could see his temples beating in his bald head.

"I think I'll go out for some fresh air," Dr. Alt said. "Care to join me?" he asked Henry.

"We have to be back in court at two o'clock," Mr. Downey said.

"We'll be there." Dr. Alt stood up. He waved his cane and said, "Lead the way, Henry."

Outside the courthouse was a fountain. Dr. Alt and Henry sat next to it. "I like fountains," the priest said. Procopius said there were fountains and aqueducts everywhere in Byzantium. Water was brought into the city from the hills and stored in cisterns and was always plentiful.

"Things aren't going too well, I hate to say." Dr. Alt laid his cane against the side of the fountain and put his hand in the water. "It's nice and cool," he said. "Father Rogan is putting up a good fight, Henry. He wants you to remain at Saint Jude's." He stirred the water with his hand. "We'll have to wait and see what happens."

People came in and out of the courthouse. Around the plaza, people were talking and sitting on the benches that ringed the fountain, reading and feeding pigeons and eating lunches from paper bags. There was lots of traffic on the street. Cars and taxis pulled up to the curb and people got in and out. Most people carried briefcases. Lots of people were wearing sunglasses.

Henry asked Dr. Alt if he had sunglasses.

"I have a pair of clip-ons," he said. "But I forgot to bring them with me. Sometimes I forget that I'm wearing them altogether. You know what's funny? Because I'm old and walk with a cane people think I'm blind and get out of the way when they see me coming."

Henry said when a blind man and one who sees are both together in darkness, they are no different from one another.

Dr. Alt chuckled and patted Henry on the cheek.

Henry said when the light comes, then he who sees will see the light and he who is blind will remain in darkness.

Dr. Alt splashed the water with his hand. "That is very profound, Henry. Is it your angel talking?"

Henry asked Dr. Alt if sunglasses were expensive.

"Some are and some aren't," Dr. Alt said. "My clip-ons sure were."

Henry asked if Dr. Alt would buy him a pair of sunglasses.

Dr. Alt took his hand out of the water and wiped it dry on his pants. "I'd be glad to, Henry. I'd be glad to. But would you do me a favor first?"

Henry asked what.

"I'd like to play a game with you."

Henry asked what game.

"A word game. I'll say a word and you say the first word that comes to mind after hearing it."

Henry said go ahead.

"Up," Dr. Alt said.

Henry said down.

"Sky."

Henry said earth.

"Man."

Henry said woman.

"Child."

Henry said mother.

"Cup."

Henry said water.

"Tree."

Henry said fruit.

"Fish."

Henry said sea.

"Dark."

Henry said light.

"One."

Henry said many.

The doctor nodded. "Every word is a sign, Henry, and signs are symbols. And symbols contain meanings."

Henry splashed more water in the fountain.

"Down, earth, woman, mother, water, fruit, sea, light, many." Dr. Alt repeated Henry's words. "The psyche contains *universes* within *universes* of meaning," Dr. Alt said. "And it is anything but innocent, and embraces every beautiful mystery." His voice trailed off and he watched Henry splash with a misty look in his eyes. Henry stopped splashing and didn't know what to do. Then, without thinking about it or knowing why, he wiped his wet hands on his pants, drew up, and gave Dr. Alt a hug. The old man was surprised but he didn't pull away. He hugged Henry back—not tightly but like a big animal playing with a smaller one. Then he reached into his pocket, took out a handkerchief, and blew his nose. For a minute Henry thought the old man was going to cry. "Can we go get sunglasses now?" he asked.

"Let's do it," the doctor said. He tucked his handkerchief back into his pocket and got to his feet.

Dr. Alt and Henry crossed the street and went into a drugstore that sold sunglasses. Henry picked out a pair. They were round with leather cups and had a string that you put around your neck. Dr. Alt said they were the kind you climbed mountains with. When Henry put them on, the store went dark green and Henry wondered if that was what *Myctophidae* saw with the lamp hanging off its nose way down at the bottom of the ocean.

When they got outside Dr. Alt said it was time to return to court. They passed in front of the big glass windows of the store and Henry saw his reflection with his new sunglasses.

"How do you like them?" Dr. Alt asked.

"They make everything look green." He now looked at the sun. It was a green disk, not a yellow ball of fire.

Dr. Alt took Henry's hand. "Now, watch where you're going," he said and they crossed the street together. When they were on the other side Dr. Alt let go of Henry's hand. "You look like Sir Edmund Hillary."

"Who is that?"

"One of the first men to climb Mount Everest."

"What is Mount Everest?"

"It's the highest mountain in the world, Henry." He lifted his cane and pointed up into the sky as if the mountain were right in front of them. Then they walked back to the courthouse.

Father Rogan and Father Crowley and Mr. Downey were waiting for them outside the courtroom.

"Where'd the sunglasses come from?" Father Crowley asked.

"I bought Henry a little present," Dr. Alt said.

"This isn't the time for giving presents," Father Rogan said. "Take off the glasses, Henry. We're going into court."

Henry shook his head.

"Don't argue with me, Henry. Take off the glasses."

Henry shook his head again.

Father Crowley reached out to take off Henry's sunglasses but Henry clamped them onto his head with both hands and turned away.

"Take off the glasses, Henry. NOW!" Father Rogan's voice echoed through the corridor. People turned to see where it came from.

Henry said he wanted to wear them.

"I'm going to count to three, Henry," Father Rogan said, and he counted to three. Then he grabbed Henry by the arm and tried to take off his glasses but Henry stomped on the priest's foot as hard as he could. Father Rogan yelled, "Ouch!" and doubled over.

Henry said he was keeping the glasses on.

Father Rogan's whole bald head went red. "I've taken about as much crap from you as I care to, young man." He reached out to grab Henry's arm but Henry bolted. The priest caught up to him at the water fountain. He grabbed his upper arm and marched him past Dr. Alt and Father Crowley and Mr. Downey straight into the court-room. When they got to their seats Father Rogan said, "Sit!"

Henry sat down and held on to his glasses with both hands and didn't look up.

Father Crowley and Dr. Alt followed them in.

"Is there a problem?" the judge asked.

"Henry refuses to remove his sunglasses, your honor."

"I can see that," the judge said. "This is a court of law, young man. Please remove the sunglasses so we can proceed."

Henry shook his head.

"Stand up," the judge told Henry.

Henry stood up but held on to his glasses with both hands and kept his head down.

"Look at me."

Henry looked up at the judge, who was leaning fo. ward with his hands clasped and his elbows spread out on the desk. There were more people in the courtroom than there had been before lunch. Theodora smiled at Henry.

"Remove the glasses," the judge said.

Henry dropped his hands to his sides but kept the sunglasses on.

The room was quiet.

"Young man, if you don't remove those glasses this instant, I will have the guard remove them for you."

A guard came over and Henry let him pluck the glasses from his face. They were attached to a string so he let them drop and Henry just stood there with the sunglasses hanging around his neck looking straight ahead like the saints looking down from the ceiling of the Hagia Sophia.

"Please sit down," the judge said.

Mr. Downey talked first. He called on Father Crowley. "I'd like you to give us your impression of the O'Brien family," he said.

Father Crowley nodded. "The O'Briens are very nice people," he said. "They seemed genuinely concerned about the boy's welfare and never interfered in my efforts to get to know him." Then he talked about their Saturday talks and told the judge about how Henry had run away the first time during school and how he had sneaked out of the rectory the second time.

Mr. Downey interrupted. "Would you say that the O'Briens provided a stable home environment for the boy?"

"Yes. I'd say so," the priest said. "But for various reasons Henry was simply not able to adjust."

Mr. Downey looked up at the judge and asked Father Crowley, "Would you say that Henry has adjusted to Saint Jude's?"

"He has appeared to."

"Thank you, Father," Mr. Downey said and then called on Father Rogan. "Would you tell us a little about Saint Jude's?" he asked.

Father Rogan began to tell the history of Saint Jude's from the beginning. He described the facilities and the routines and the responsibilities and the educational opportunities each boy was offered. The judge interrupted. "It sounds like an impressive institution, Father," he said. "But I'm afraid our time is limited."

"I understand, your honor," Father Rogan said. Then he talked about the individual attention that each boy received. He began naming boys who had left Saint Jude's and become famous, starting with the most famous one, who worked for the president of the United States and got his name in the newspapers almost every day.

Theodora's lawyer interrupted. "I object, your honor. I don't see how the names of alumni are relevant here."

The judge let Father Rogan continue.

Father Rogan talked for a little while about the philosophy of Saint Jude's.

The judge interrupted. "Thank you, Father. Briefly, could you state why you think Henry should remain at Saint Jude's?"

Father Rogan looked down for a moment and the lights in the ceiling flashed off his bald head. He took out a handkerchief and patted the back of his neck and wiped his brow. "It's my opinion, your honor, as a priest and an educator, that a hotel casino in Atlantic City is no place for a child to grow up." He spoke very slowly and deliberately. "Especially since the boy has already lived there and seems to have been exposed to some rather—shall we say unseemly?—things." He looked at Theodora. "Henry seems to have some rather special *gifts*. I think it would be appropriate to call them that. At any rate, the nature of his gifts makes it even more imperative that he be placed in an appropriate environment. For the life of me, I can't imagine how the moral and spiritual aspects of Henry's education could be advanced in the atmosphere of one of the biggest gambling hotels in the country." He wiped his head again. "That's all I have to say, your honor."

The judge wrote down some things and everyone in the room was quiet. Then he told Theodora's lawyer to proceed. The man behind the briefcase stood up and touched his pen to his lips as though he were still thinking about what to say. Then he called on Farley. "As Henry's probation officer, could you please tell us about your last visit to Saint Jude's?"

Farley stood up and explained that she had gone to Saint Jude's with a representative of the adoption agency and a state social worker.

"You all saw Henry during the visit?"

"We did, yes."

"Describe the circumstances, please."

"Well, we were taken into the director's office. Henry was brought in by a staff member."

"Could you describe Henry's appearance?"

"He appeared to have been badly beaten."

Father Rogan tried to stand up but Mr. Downey pulled him back into his seat.

"Describe Henry's appearance."

"He had a large bruise on one side of his face." She traced a line under her own eye. "His cheek was badly swollen. Also, it looked to me like his nose might have been broken."

Father Rogan stood up. "Excuse me, your honor. This is a total exaggeration. Nothing was broken."

"Please, Father," the judge said.

"Did you ask what happened?"

"Yes," Farley said. "May I read from my notes?"

The judge nodded.

Farley flipped open a small notebook she was holding. "The answer was, quote, 'Some of the older boys got rough with him, unquote."

"Is that all you were told?"

"It is," Farley said.

"Were you satisfied with the answer?"

"No, sir. I was not," Farley said. "I had the feeling that it wasn't being taken very seriously."

"In what way?"

"Well, like we weren't being told everything."

"Are you a mother?" Theodora's lawyer asked Farley.

"I have two children."

Theodora's lawyer folded his hands together and held them in front of his mouth like he was about to say something that he really didn't want to say. Mr. Downey leaned over and whispered to Father Rogan. Dr. Alt took Henry's hand and held it. Nobody stirred. Even his angel was silent. Henry felt the whole courtroom staring at him.

Farley went on talking. Henry just sat there between the two priests and played with the sunglasses around his neck. He looked over at Theodora now and then because she was sitting there quietly and not saying anything. He tried to imagine his mother and his angel began to talk again. Its voice was like a whisper because all secrets must be whispered and Henry thought about his visit to prison where all the whispers were drowned out by the shouting and clamoring of the prisoners and he understood that being in prison was like being whispered in a secret. Being in prison meant being in the shadow of the light. It meant coming forth into the air from the invisible mother and hardening through her hardness. As a saint, Henry knew that being in the world meant passing from prison to prison.

Then the yelling began. Father Rogan and Mr. Downey were yelling at Theodora's lawyer. The judge was banging his hammer and saying, "Come to order. Come to order." Father Rogan started telling the judge that Theodora's lawyer was making outrageous insinuations and his tactics were despicable. Henry didn't listen to the fighting; he was trying to hear his angel. Then Dr. Alt took him by the hand and led him out of the courtroom.

"There's no need for us to sit through all this," he said.

Henry put on his sunglasses and they went into a big room that was filled with people watching TV and reading newspapers and magazines. "I'm exhausted," Dr. Alt said. He sat down and held his cane between his knees and patted Henry's shoulder. He took off his glasses and rubbed his eyes. "I'm just completely exhausted."

A little while later they went back into the courtroom because it was Dr. Alt's turn to talk. While he talked everyone in the room was quiet. Even the lawyers didn't try to interrupt him. He told the judge about his impression when he first met Henry and then about how it changed after his later talks with him. "I would be glad to explain my opinion. But it's rather technical."

The judge nodded.

Dr. Alt took off his glasses and cleaned them. "First of all, it must be understood that *analytical* psychology rests upon the premise that the unconscious is the habitus of ancestral psychic life and that it is made up of several elements, each of which has separate and autonomous functions. These separate elements of the unconscious must maintain a certain relationship to each other to produce what we call *normality* in the psychological sense." He stopped to let these comments sink in, then continued. "Now, in analytical psychology, the *ego* is defined as the complex of factors made of all *conscious* contents. It is the center of consciousness and makes up the *empirical* personality—in the sense that the ego is the subject of all conscious acts. The *self* is not to be confused with the ego. The self encompasses all aspects of the conscious *and* unconscious personality, and thus contains and even defines the ego." He drew a circle in the air with his finger. "This is the self." He drew a smaller circle inside it. "This is the ego." He poked his finger into it as though he were popping a balloon. Then he looked around the room as though he wanted someone to ask a question. But nobody did, so he continued. "The more numerous and significant the *unconscious* contents which are assimilated by the ego, the closer the approximation of the ego to the self." He let his cane fall against his chair and cupped his hands in the air and spread them apart. "This produces an *inflation* of the ego—unless a critical line of demarcation is drawn between it and the unconscious figures."

The courtroom was still quiet. Everyone was watching the old priest but nobody said anything and nobody asked any questions. Only the judge looked interested. Henry put his sunglasses on but Father Rogan took them off and forced Henry's hand into his lap and held it there.

Dr. Alt kept talking. "What I am describing here is nothing less than a psychic *catastrophe*." He paused for a few seconds and looked around and still nobody interrupted him. "When the ego is assimilated by the self with no *boundaries* fixed to it—in other words, when the normal frontier between the conscious and unconscious is *erased* and the figures of the unconscious migrate into the conscious and remain there—the result could be described as a sort of permanent hallucination of the inner life, a somatic dream state." He made a balloon in the air with his hands again. "The time-space continuum in which the conscious mind functions is invaded by the *archaic* elements of the unconscious." He spread his hands wide as though the balloon he was holding was being inflated. "The absolute time and space which the conscious psyche inhabits is *annihilated*." Then he clapped his hands together loudly—POP POP! Everyone in the courtroom jumped.

"I'm sorry to interrupt," the judge said. "Your testimony is extremely interesting. A little technical, but very interesting. In your opinion, is the boy's condition severe enough to require institutionalization?"

"No. Absolutely not."

"Are there any reasons why he should *not* be able to live in a normal family situation?"

"There aren't," Dr. Alt said. "But the *peculiarity* of his condition might make it difficult for him."

"May I ask what your recommendation would be? As a doctor, I mean."

Dr. Alt glanced at the other priests. "Saint Jude's seems to suit Henry well, from what I have observed. He seems happy there. And, of course, the place is well equipped to meet his special needs."

"Thank you, Father," the judge said and left the room while he made his decision.

They stood on the steps of the courthouse. Theodora's lawyer put his briefcase down and loosened his tie. Then a blue Mercedes 500 SEL pulled up. "Here we are," Theodora said and they went down the steps. Theodora and Henry sat in the back seat together. The lawyer sat up front with the driver. Suddenly the three priests appeared and the driver opened the windows automatically. Father Rogan put his hand in and patted Henry's cheek. Father Crowley made the sign of the cross over him and said he would remember Henry in his prayers. Dr. Alt leaned on his cane and looked sad and said nothing.

"Let's get going," Theodora said to the driver.

The three priests waved as they drove away.

Henry looked out the window for a while as they drove along the highway. Philadelphia was a dirty place when you looked at it from the highway overpasses.

Buildings fell down and weeds grew out of them. The ships and storage tanks in the harbor were all rusty and old. It wasn't like Byzantium at all. Procopius said Byzantium sparkled and so did everyone who lived there. He said when monuments and buildings got old and dirty or if they fell down, the emperor sent people to clean them up. If something burned down or was knocked down by an earthquake, the emperor rebuilt it even better than it was before. If his warships got old or were damaged in battles on the sea, the emperor destroyed them and built new ones. The emperor took care of his city like it was his only child.

Theodora and the lawyer talked but Henry didn't listen to what they were saying. He thought about how she smiled when the judge read his decision. It wasn't happy or mean but something in between, like the smile of someone confident in victory and content with beauty of a lower order. She looked over to where Henry and the priests were sitting. Henry looked back at her but the priests didn't. He remembered how beautifully she swam in the Olympic pool and how whenever he saw her at the Palace—walking here and there in a hurry to get things done—he wished secretly to be noticed by her and have her love him, and how, when he learned that his father hated her, he began to feel afraid whenever he saw her—not because he hated her but because his father did—and how he then started to hate her too and hid whenever he saw her coming because he was afraid.

Henry rolled down the window and put his sunglasses on. Theodora reached across the seat and took his hand. He started to pull it back but she held it tightly, so he let her have it and poked his head out of the speeding car. He watched the mile markers flit past on the side of the highway. He listened to the rush of the wind in his ears and the roar of cars and trucks. His angel said everything that is bound together eventually comes unbound, and even a mother and her child are not much different than cars passing each other on a busy highway.

When they arrived at the Palace Theodora took Henry up to the penthouse and into the kitchen and introduced him to Antonia. Antonia was an old woman. Sy used to call her the oldest whore in Christendom because she sometimes appeared downstairs dressed up with big feathers and gloves that ran all the way up her arms. Sometimes she played blackjack at Sy's table. He liked to say that the only thing older than Christendom itself was the sight of an old whore playing the tables.

The kitchen was big and had a balcony with trees in pots and a table and chairs. Antonia was watering.

"This is Henry, Antonia."

Antonia held out a knobby hand. "Pleased to meet you, young man."

"Antonia is in charge of everything up here," Theodora said. "If you ever need anything, just ask her." Then she told Antonia she was going to show Henry his room and asked her to pour some lemonade for them.

They went to his room and Theodora opened all the closets and drawers to show him where all his new clothes were. She made him sit down at the desk in the corner. "For doing homework," she said. She showed him his bathroom. "It's your responsibility to keep your room clean, Henry. Antonia is too old to be cleaning up after little boys."

Henry said he wanted his books.

"I'll make sure all your things are sent." She smiled and looked around the room as if it were the fulfillment of a secret wish. "I hope you'll like living here," she said.

Henry said thank you. The Samaritan gave nothing but wine and oil to the wounded man.

Theodora looked at Henry for a moment. "There's lemonade for us in the kitchen," she said. He followed her out of the room and down the hall that led to the kitchen. "I don't want you thanking me for anything, Henry," she said. "Ever." She didn't turn around or stop walking when she said it but just kept straight on into the kitchen, where her heels made a sharp clicking noise when she walked.

From Theodora's kitchen you could see to the ends of the city and far out to sea. Antonia put two glasses of lemonade on the table and asked Theodora if they wanted anything to eat.

Theodora shook her head. "Do you still remember your way around?" she asked Henry.

Henry said some things were different than before.

"That's very true," Theodora said. "There's a lot of construction going on. Why don't you tell me about Saint Jude's? It sounds to me like a pretty rough place."

Henry said nothing.

"I know about the problems you've had. I understand if you don't want to talk about them." She took a sip of lemonade and stared at Henry over the rim of the glass. Then she put the glass down. "I want you to feel comfortable and at home here, Henry. I also want you to feel that you can talk to me about anything."

Henry took a sip of lemonade and the angel in his ear said if you love it, it will paralyze you. Henry didn't spit out the lemonade because he knew the angel wasn't talking about the drink but about Theodora. He looked at her and tried to see himself in her the way he thought he might see himself in his mother. He wondered why she had brought him to live with her.

Henry thought about his father. Only the father of a saint would know enough to abandon him. When you made something you had to leave it alone when it was finished. That's what Sy said about God and horse racing and now that's what Henry remembered whenever he thought about his father. He asked his angel where his father was.

The angel said his father had forsaken him but that Henry would be reunited with him the way truth was reunited with ignorance and the soul with the body at the end of the world.

Theodora looked past Henry out the window. She sat slumped with one elbow on the back of her chair, her other arm on the table and all the secrets of her nature carefully sealed within. Sy told Henry once that keeping secrets made you strong and telling secrets made you weak. He used to say if you want to keep a friend, keep a secret. He said it all the time, which meant Sy probably didn't have any friends or any secrets. Henry's father didn't have any friends either, but he did have many secrets—and now that was all he had. Henry wondered why his father hated Theodora. She had let them stay in the Palace and that's just what Henry's father wanted. Was that why he hated her? Because she had let him have just what he wanted? Henry looked at Theodora to see what it was that his father had hated. All he saw was a dark-haired woman with a square jaw and a blue suit and a string of pearls and a gold watch and lines around her mouth and eyes that meant she got angry a lot and probably couldn't sleep. He wanted to ask her why she had brought him to live with her—but he couldn't, so he looked out the big glass sliding door and across the blue ocean, where right now whales were swimming beneath the surface. Being high up in the penthouse meant seeing far into the distance. Being high up in the penthouse was like having all of Byzantium laid at your feet.

"I'm having a special guest for dinner tonight," Theodora said. "You're going to eat with us." She stood up and finished her glass of lemonade. "Would you help me set the table?"

Henry followed her into the dining room, which had a wall of windows overlooking the ocean. The penthouse was shaped like a giant star on the top of the Palace and every room opened onto a patio. The dining room and the living room had glass walls and a garden between them with lots of plants and walkways and even a pond with goldfish in it. At the far edge of the garden you could see the other tall buildings thrown up along the coastline.

Theodora opened a drawer and picked out some knives and forks and spoons and handed them to Henry. She opened another drawer and took out some linen and told Henry where to put everything. Then she put glasses at each place and explained that one was for water and the other for wine and even though Henry was too young for wine, that was how you set a table properly. She went into the next room and came back with a big vase full of flowers and put it on the table between two tall candles and she stood back and crossed her arms and said it looked nice.

A man came in wheeling a silver cart.

"Put it over there, Larry," Theodora told him and pointed to a place along the wall of the dining room. "And say hello to Henry."

"Hello, Henry," Larry said.

"Say hello to Larry, Henry," Theodora said. "You're going to be seeing a lot of him. He's the butler."

Henry said hello.

Larry was dressed up in a monkey suit. That's what Sy used to call them. Larry smoothed out the tablecloth and rearranged a few things. He had big muscles and a nice voice. Henry didn't remember him from before. He must have just come to the Palace. "Should I bring up some wine?" he asked.

"Some chardonnay for me," Theodora said. "I don't think anyone else will care for wine." Then she told Henry to go get dressed and get ready to meet their guest.

From the window of his room Henry could see in the direction of the Golden Horn. He could see the buildings the emperor had built, including the Hagia Sophia and the Senate and other new buildings that had risen out of the destruction caused by the riots. They were bigger and more magnificent and also more severe than the old buildings that had once made the city a more comfortable place to live. Instead of wood they were built with stone and glass. Their names were Balley's and Trump and Tropicana and Taj and helicopters could land on their roofs and people came and went through large doors that swallowed them and spat them out again.

Henry buttoned up his shirt and listened to his angel. The angel said the world came about through a mistake, which meant everything in the world was also a mistake— including the way Henry buttoned his shirt. It was warm outside, and light. The other hotels were all closed up behind glass windows and lighted signs that never went off. The signs stayed on so people from other parts of the empire and foreign visitors could know where they were.

There were people from everywhere, not just Greeks and Romans but Cappadocians and Phrygians and Goths and Celts and Armenians and Copts and Syrians and Jews and Franks and Huns and Gepids and Avars and Sarmatians and Bulimics.

Theodora knocked on the door and came in. She saw Henry standing in front of the mirror in the clothes she had given him. "My, you look handsome!" She stood next to him and combed his hair to one side with her fingers. They stood there together for a minute just looking at their reflections in the mirror. Theodora rested her hand on Henry's shoulder. She was wearing a ring with a huge diamond that sparkled cruelly, as if her hand were something that could do or undo anything she wanted. Henry watched the diamond sparkle while Theodora judged their appearance in the mirror. "Our dinner guest is here. Come in and say hello." She took Henry by the hand and led him to the living room.

The emperor was sitting on the sofa. He looked exactly like before except the bright lights made him look pale and white and the big sofa made him look small. He had big brown freckles on his head and was wearing a white shirt that had a little design on it.

"Say hello, Henry," Theodora said.

Henry said hello.

"Hello, Henry," the emperor said and motioned for Henry to come sit by him. Henry went and sat on the sofa—not next to the emperor but at the other end. "Come closer, son." He patted the cushion. "There's nothing to be afraid of."

Henry moved closer but still didn't sit next to the emperor. Theodora went over to the big window and adjusted the curtains.

"How do you like your new home?" the emperor asked.

Henry said it was all right. Then his angel said the veil at first concealed how God ordered the creation, but when the veil is rent and the things within become visible this house will be left deserted and will be destroyed.

The emperor stared at Henry and didn't say anything. Henry could hear him breathing and he wondered if the old man was sick. In the Palace there were machines that told you your weight and your fortune, your mood and your fortune, and your blood pressure and your fortune. All you had to do was put a coin in and step onto a scale or put your finger into a metal loop. Henry wondered if the emperor needed to go use one of those machines. "Do you remember me?" the emperor finally asked. "You came to visit me once."

Henry nodded his head but didn't say anything. Theodora was standing over by the sliding glass door that led outside. Her eyes were sparkling like the diamond on her finger. "I hope you don't mind if we sit right down to eat," she said.

The emperor waved his arm. "Please."

Theodora led the way to the table. Larry was standing behind a silver cart. He gestured for the emperor to sit at the head of the table. Theodora sat on the emperor's right and Henry sat on his left in a chair with a booster seat.

"Would you care for wine?" Larry asked the emperor.

The emperor shook his head. "Just my usual," he said.

Larry poured the emperor some fizzy water from a green bottle that said *Apollonaris* on it. It didn't look like anything an emperor or a god would drink. It looked like medicine.

"I'll have wine," Theodora said. Larry took a bottle wrapped in a white cloth from a bucket. He poured wine into Theodora's glass.

"What would you like to drink, Henry?" Larry asked.

Henry said water and Larry got a glass pitcher and filled Henry's glass. The water had ice in it and Henry counted the cubes. There were seven. Then he looked up at the emperor and asked if his father got the job.

The emperor frowned. He took a sip of his fizzy water and put the glass down. "I'm not sure I know what you're talking about, son," he said.

Theodora had a funny look on her face. "Would you mind explaining, Henry?"

Henry said the job his father had asked for when they came to visit. Did the emperor give it to him?

The emperor wrinkled his forehead and his eyes opened wide. "Ah, *that*," he said and shook his head. "I'm afraid not, son. As a matter of fact, he didn't even wait around to find out. He just—well, he just disappeared." He looked at Theodora.

Theodora nodded. "That's right, Henry. That's why I brought you here. To take care of you and keep you safe."

The emperor said, "Son, your father committed a serious crime and absconded. Do you know what *absconded* means?"

Henry said it meant that he escaped through a hole in the darkness and into another darkness.

Theodora smiled and took a sip of her wine.

The emperor shook his head. "You're too young to understand, son. When you're older, that's when you'll understand."

"Try not to think about it too much," Theodora said. "What's important now is that you're safe and sound." She reached across the table and tried to take Henry's hand but he moved away.

Just then Larry came in with three small salads and set one down in front of each of them. "Bon appetit," he said and poured more wine into Theodora's glass.

The emperor picked up his fork. "Have you ever been up in a helicopter?" he asked Henry.

Henry shook his head.

"They're fun," Theodora said. "Helicopter tours! We'll take one tomorrow. Would you like that?"

Henry said nothing.

"You can see the *whole* coastline," the emperor said.

Henry said I have cast the beam out of my own eye and now see clearly enough to cast the mote from the eye of my brother.

The emperor made a funny face and Theodora laughed. Her laugh didn't sound like it came from deep inside but from someplace behind her nose. Then the emperor put his fork down and took some bread from the basket on the table. He began to eat but his frown didn't go away and he took another sip of fizzy water.

"There's nothing to worry about," Theodora said. She took a tiny sip of her wine.

The emperor didn't say anything and didn't look up from his plate.

"I don't want anyone to be unhappy or to worry," Theodora said. She looked at the emperor and at Henry. "Everything is going to turn out just fine."

The emperor kept eating and didn't say anything. He moaned very quietly as he chewed. He began to slump in his chair a little and it made him look somehow sad and unhappy. Then he put his fork down, took his napkin, and wiped his mouth. Larry appeared right away. He took the empty plates and put new ones in front of them. The emperor began to eat and nobody said anything for a few minutes. Then he saw that Henry wasn't eating. "What's wrong?" he asked. "You don't like chicken?"

Henry shook his head.

The emperor shook his head. "You're too young to be turning your nose up at good food, young man." He popped a piece of bread into his mouth and looked at Henry as he chewed. "Come on, now. Eat."

Henry felt his ears burning. Then his angel began to talk. Henry sat there looking at the old emperor and Theodora and they seemed to him like mute facades inhabited by some mysterious indisposition. He wasn't hungry and couldn't eat and didn't want to talk or answer questions anymore. He wished he could go back to Saint Jude's. He slid off his chair and his napkin fell on the floor. He walked away without picking it up.

"Come back here, young man," the emperor said. "You haven't been excused."

"That's all right," Theodora said. "Let him go."

Some kids were afraid of the dark. Henry guessed they were afraid because they couldn't see what it contained. They were afraid because it swallowed them and when you were swallowed by darkness you were cut off from everything else—even your parents. Parents were no good in the dark. They were part of the light. If you took your parents with you into the dark they were no longer your parents. But if you suddenly found yourself in the light and someone was next to you holding your hand, that person was your parent and when they disappeared whoever took their place was your parent and on and on in one direction until the beginning and in the other direction until the end of the world, where you found yourself standing next to the one God, who had left you to your own devices.

He went to his room and began to cry. He stood in front of the mirror and saw his new clothes, his whole self and his self apart. He turned toward the window that looked out upon his two cities, which were also two entities yet one form. Atlantic City. Byzantium. Everything resolved itself in twos, even Henry's angel, who was both silent and not silent at the same time and who drove Henry's thoughts and was driven by them. The angel said everything in twos would dissolve into its earliest origin. Henry tried to think of his own earliest origin but the earliest he could remember was the time when he and his father had lived in the apartment with Ten Cents a Dance. Further back was only darkness.

At last he stopped crying. He wiped his eyes with the back of his hand and looked up. His angel was standing next to him. It had big wings that arched high up and towered over them both. They were thick with soft, transparent feathers and the tips almost touched the ground. They were real wings. Wings to fly with, wings to soar. Henry was not afraid. He looked into the angel's face. It was the face of a man and a woman and a friend with a door that opens at every knock. Henry closed his eyes. Antonia was making noise in the kitchen and he could hear the wind outside and the hum of all the floors of the vented building underneath him. He thought of Father Crowley and Dr. Alt and Father Rogan and Sy and his father and the Whore of Jersey City and Helena and her baby and Mohammed Ali and Mr. and Mrs. O'Brien. The darkness felt good. Henry followed his angel toward it and together they dissolved into their earliest origins.

Theodora came into Henry's room and sat on the edge of the bed. She didn't say anything for a while but just sat there with her legs crossed and her hands on her knee. "What can I do to help you be less angry?" she finally asked.

Henry said I have cast fire upon the world and I am guarding it until it blazes.

"I don't understand you, Henry. You'll have to think of another way of expressing yourself to me."

Henry said nothing.

"Where did you learn to say such things?"

Henry said nothing.

"Is that how they talk at Saint Jude's?"

Henry said no.

"Where did you learn to talk like that?"

Henry said an angel taught him.

Theodora stood up and walked over to the window and stood there. Behind her the city blinked, walls of little lights stacked up on top of and beside one another against the blackness. The diamond on her hand sparkled as though the sun were shining on it. She leaned against the windowsill. She was tall and lean and looked different up close than she did gliding through the water of the swim-

ming pool. She looked old, and Henry remembered that
his father had always said she was older than she looked
and that she used her power like an old man does—to
keep people in their places and at a safe distance. "Maybe
we should get things right out in the open," she said. "Put
all our cards on the table."

Cards made Henry think about Sy but as soon as he
did he wished he hadn't because now Sy was gone.

"I can't force you to be happy. But I promise that I will
always be frank with you. I hope, at the very least, you
will respect me for that." She paused for a minute and
looked down at the floor. "You know that your father has
done a terrible thing."

Henry asked what his father did that was terrible.

"He stole. He cheated. He lied. Worst of all, he abandoned you, his own helpless child."

Henry focused his eyes on the blinking lights outside.
Theodora's features became blurry and hardened at the
same time. "I'm not trying to make you any sadder than
you already are. Do you understand that?"

Henry said nothing.

"I'm not trying to hurt you either. Or cause you any
more pain than you've already suffered. Are you listening
to me?"

Henry tried not to cry.

"Would you like me to explain why I brought you
here?"

Henry nodded.

"Okay, Henry," she said. "The reason is because I want to protect you. I don't want to see you suffer any more than you already have. Together you and I will stand up against what your father has done. He will have to face up to what he did to *you* by facing up to *me;* and he'll have to face up to what he did to *me* when he faces up to *you*." She came over and sat down on the bed again. "We need to stick together. Does that make any sense to you?"

Henry said nothing.

"One day—even if he's never caught—your father will have to come to terms with what he has done. He might have put himself beyond our reach and the reach of the law, but he hasn't put himself beyond the reach of his own conscience. When he is ready to confront *that*—we'll be waiting for him." She poked her finger into the mattress. "Right here. You and I. The both of us, together."

The room was dark except for the light in the bathroom that laid a streak across the floor and climbed up the far wall. Theodora stood up. "I'm going to take good care of you, Henry. And as long as we are together, your father will not get away." She stood there in the streak of light and Henry remembered the days when he would watch her swimming; now she was standing right in front of him, not dripping wet but lit up and sparkling with jewels. "Good night," she said and quietly left the room.

A while later Antonia came into Henry's room. "Come into the kitchen and I'll fix you a snack," she said. She was wearing an old robe that hung down to her ankles and her gray hair was loose and hung down around her shoulders. It made her look decrepit.

Henry was sitting up in the bed. He said he didn't want anything.

"Can I come in for a minute?"

Henry said okay.

Antonia came in and looked around. "We fixed the room up just for you," she said and turned on the desk lamp. "Do you like it?"

Henry nodded.

"Theodora wants you to like her and feel at home," the old woman said. "She wants that very badly."

Henry said nothing.

"She works very hard. Too hard, if you ask me. She never had a family of her own. I think she's lonely."

Henry said what about her husband.

Antonia shook her head and gave Henry a funny look. "It's been a rough day," she said and stood up. "If you get hungry in the middle of the night there's a piece of apple pie in the fridge. Help yourself."

Henry lay in bed and waited in the darkness until all he could hear was the quiet humming of the building. Then he opened the door and tiptoed out into the hall. At the far end of the hallway was a door with a key in the lock. Henry turned the key and opened the door. A staircase led down into darkness. He felt along the wall for a switch but couldn't find one. Then he heard a sound like a door opening and he stepped through the door and closed it behind him. It was pitch black.

Henry tried to see through the darkness but his eyes didn't help him. He felt the top step with his foot and took one step down. Then he sat on the top step and did tushie pops—Helena had taught him how to do tushie pops—pop, pop, pop, step by step down into the darkness. He came to a landing, crawled around to a second set of steps, and then slid down them until he saw a light switch glowing in the blackness below him. He descended into the blackness and when he reached the bottom he turned on the switch and found himself facing a door at the bottom of the staircase. He pushed it open and walked into a brightly lit corridor. He ran to the end of the corridor and called the elevator. On the elevator were a man and a woman who were holding drinks in their hands. "A little past your bedtime, isn't it, kid?" the man said.

Henry stared at the panel of buttons and didn't say anything.

The man put his arm around the woman and whispered something in her ear. It sounded like he said crazy parents or something but Henry didn't really hear. The woman shook her head and looked away.

When the doors opened Henry walked straight through the lobby, where people were still coming and going and laughing and talking, through the revolving door at the entrance. There were taxis and cars and people were standing around in groups. Then he felt the night air on his face and heard the thrumming of the ocean and smelled its smell. He ran as fast as he could down the lighted boardwalk.

He stayed in the shadows on his way to the water. Procopius said the streets of Byzantium were crowded late at night with groups and factions. Most were coming from the games and were still charged by the glory of their color. It didn't matter if Blue or Green had won; their supporters tumbled through the streets and shouted and sang and made the night noisy. Sy used to tell Henry the city was great because it devoted as much energy to the night as it did to the day, and when Henry was clear of the shadow of Caesar's Palace he knew he was safe because now it would be hard to find him in all the clattering.

The ocean was calm and he stood at the water's edge, where everything stretched out forever. Sometimes the dead were carried across the water standing up in long boats and sometimes they rose up into the air and their spirits made an invisible trail across the sky and sometimes they just woke up disoriented in a place without a name. He felt the breeze blow through his hair and the water splashing up the backs of his legs. He stooped and lifted a handful of wet sand and let it dribble through his fingers. He took the chain from around his neck, the chain his father had given him, and held it in his sandy palm. Gold was heavier than sand, but as it dribbled through his fingers it felt no different. He watched as the surf washed over it, a sliver of gold glimmering in the foam. Then, just as it was about to disappear, he snatched it up and put it on again.

Rising up into the night sky were all the dizzy lights of the city. He could see Caesar's Palace and Balley's Wild West and Trump Plaza and the Tropicana and the Taj Mahal and the Hagia Sophia and the golden statue on top of the Column of Constantine. In the days when he came down to the water with Helena, Henry would try to see how far he could walk along the shore before the city vanished into the horizon. He never made it far enough to escape the sights and the smells and the sounds of the city but when his father brought him out to the beach and told him he had to leave the Palace, they walked so far that even the tallest buildings looked like small huts on the shore. That day everything receded and became like decorations floating in the middle distances. The middle distances are the places where the things you can't take with you have to be left, the places where nothing originates. Henry and his father walked farther away from the city than Henry had ever walked before and when they returned to the Palace Henry's father told him to pack up his gear and be ready to leave first thing in the morning.

It grew darker and darker and Henry walked and walked and went way past everything. When he turned to look, the city twinkled in the distance like something on top of a cake. He watched it twinkle for a while and his angel began to talk but Henry paid no attention. Instead he listened to the waves breaking on the shore and tried to hear the underlying voices of the ocean, but after trying and trying to decipher the crashing and tumbling and hissing he gave up and continued walking. His feet sank into the wet sand. His angel continued talking. Henry forced himself not to listen and he tried to concentrate on the smells in the air and the feel of the breeze against his skin. He sat down and took off his sneakers and dug his feet and hands into the sand. He tried to concentrate simultaneously on the feeling of all the grains of sand together and the feeling of each one apart and he fingered the chain around his neck and promised that he would always keep it no matter what and that it would always remind him of his father. He looked up at the stars and thought of them as the sand's counterpart in heaven, and his angel put the image in his mind of a beach up there and sitting on that beach another Henry with another angel in his ear and a chain around his neck and stars spilling from his hands and his feet dug underneath a trillion suns. But then it all collapsed. That Henry was merely vaster. In the great conflation of names and things that make up the world, being more vast only means being supported by a greater nothingness. Instead of wishing he were identical to the cosmic Henry, the Henry on the beach wished both would just disappear. In the vastness of the world, the scale of loneliness is constant and can never be divided. Loneliness is the most meaningless treasure in existence.

Henry watched the moon rise. He tried to imagine his self and his self apart fulfilling all the duties of a saint. The first thing he would do would be to bless and forgive all the people he had ever known or who had ever known him. Even the drunken couple in the elevator. Henry's angel said only through this perversion of forgiving can the perversion that is the world be transformed into the eternal realm. His angel also said that none shall be able to torment him even while he dwells in the world because a saint has had the light revealed to him and the light is the truth and the truth is what makes you free.

Across the water the limitless darkness of the night sky met the limitless churning of the ocean. Henry saw that where the two met was also the place where the beginning and the end came together. Not in the neat line of the horizon but in the jagged edges of chaos. You needed light to see the neat line of the horizon, but you needed secret knowledge to see the jagged edges of chaos. A saint had to know these things. A saint had to know that Creator and creation are separate and distinct and that the one does not recognize itself in the other. They can never know each other. They can never be united. Reunions do not happen. A child cannot return to the mother, nor the mother to her mother, and dissolve all creation backward to the beginning. A saint had to know that the chains that bind each child to life will one day break but that it doesn't matter because *once it was it will have been forever*. Most important of all, a saint had to know that knowing all this did not bring anything nearer to its origins. Everything that *is* originated in something *else* that could not be known. A mother was a mother and the child of the mother was the mother's child and they were other and separate and alien.

In Atlantic City the biggest buildings were built along the shore. They were always noisy and never still. Henry walked and walked and walked along the beach until the moon was almost directly overhead. Then, when the city was not even a pinprick of light on the horizon, he turned and walked back to Caesar's Palace. He wondered how it was that such a busy place—a place where there was nothing but playing and shouting and carrying on all day and all night, a place that was both the starting point and the destination of so many simultaneous voyages, a place where east toucheth west, ocean toucheth land, a rock toucheth a hard place—could also seem so calm? And when his angel finally left him, Henry understood that it was always like that wherever one thing ended and something else began.

14

R 61
16⅓

28 Day Loan